P9-DIY-864

DISNEP

MALEFICENT

DISNEY
MALEFICENT

Adapted by Elizabeth Rudnick

Based on the screenplay by Linda Woolverton

Executive Producers Angelina Jolie, Don Hahn,
Palak Patel, Matt Smith, Sarah Bradshaw

Produced by Joe Roth

Directed by Robert Stromberg

DISNEY PRESS
New York • Los Angeles

Special thanks to Brittany Candau.

Copyright © 2014 Disney Enterprises, Inc.

All rights reserved. Published by Disney Press, an imprint of
Disney Book Group. No part of this book may be reproduced or
transmitted in any form or by any means, electronic or mechanical,
including photocopying, recording, or by any information storage and
retrieval system, without written permission from the publisher.
For information, address Disney Press, 1101 Flower Street,
Glendale, California 91201.

Printed in the United States of America
First Edition
3 5 7 9 10 8 6 4
G475-5664-5-14157
Library of Congress Control Number: 2013946498

ISBN 978-1-4231-8543-7

disneybooks.com

disney.com/maleficent

THIS LABEL APPLIES TO TEXT STOCK

For L.W.

THIS IS THE STORY OF THE FAERIE MALEFICENT. NOT THE STORY YOU THINK YOU KNOW. NOT THE ONE THAT STARTS WITH A CURSE AND ENDS WITH A DRAGON. NO. THIS IS WHAT REALLY HAPPENED. And while it may have a curse and a dragon, it has much more. For it is a story of lost love, found friendships, and, ultimately, the power of a single kiss. . . .

PROLOGUE—
SCOTTISH HIGHLANDS

LATE AFTERNOON SUN FILTERED ACROSS A WIDE EXPANSE OF THICK GRASS, TURNING THE GREEN BLADES GOLDEN. IN THE SKY, CLOUDS MOVED SLOWLY, THEIR UNHURRIED MOVEMENTS MIMICKING THE FLUFFY WHITE SHEEP IN THE FIELD BELOW. Sitting on a nearby stone wall, a shepherd and his four-year-old son kept watch over their flock. At their feet sat two collies, their eyes closed as they relaxed from their watchdog duties for a moment.

This was the young boy's first trip to the pasture with his father. He had waited for this day forever, always the one left behind while his brothers took the flocks farther and farther afield. But now it was his turn. He had run behind his father the whole way, trying not to scare the sheep when they finally found them at the back of one of the farthest fields. Then he had hooted and hol-lered, mimicking his father as best he could, to make the furry creatures move on.

With all the new experiences and all the running and yelling, the boy had worked up quite the appetite. Supper had been quickly devoured, and now he took a big bite of his sweet cake. Crumbs fell onto his lap as he enjoyed the treat. Noticing his father had placed his own treat on the ground next to him, the young boy cocked his head. "You don't want your sweet cake, Papa?" he asked.

"I'm leaving it there for the Fair Folk," the shepherd answered, his weathered face serious.

Wasting a treat? The young boy had never heard of such a thing. "Why?" he asked.

Smiling at his son's inquisitive nature, the father answered, "To thank them for making the grass grow tall and helping the flowers bloom. To show that we mean them no harm."

But that was not enough of an answer for the boy. He had more questions. "Why do they do that? What would we harm them for?" he asked, his tiny voice full of confusion.

Before saying anything, the shepherd smoothed the dirt beneath him with his worn boot. The soles were brown with the earth of the fields, and the tips were faded. Times had been tough of late, with King Henry demanding more and more of their crops and sheep every year. Things like boots, hope, and dirt were what the farmer held on to tight now. "They're part of nature. They care to the plants, the animals, even the air itself," he went on as he scooped up a handful of loose dirt and slowly made a soil wreath around the treat. "But not all humans appreciate them. Some people attack their land, wanting to reap the benefits of all their natural treasures. Aye, there have been many pointless wars between greedy humans and the Fair Folk. And no matter how many times both sides strive for peace, we always seem to be on the brink of another." The shepherd looked into the distance wistfully.

This was too much for the boy to handle. His father was talking gibberish! Whenever *he* said silly things, his mother would cuff him upside the head and send him out to the barn to clean the stalls. But since he couldn't do that to his own father, he just asked, "Why are you doing that with the dirt?"

"It is a sign of respect," the father answered matter-of-factly. "We want the Fair Folk to know it is safe for them to eat it. We don't want them thinking we've tried to poison them. Faeries can be quite mean if they are provoked." Standing up, he whistled to the dogs and began to walk home.

Behind him, the boy sat on the wall, his mind racing. He had never heard of *mean* faeries. Looking nervously over his shoulder, he scanned the large wall. Not satisfied that he wasn't being watched by mean faeries, he jumped off the stones. Then, uttering a soft cry, he raced after his father. When he was safely by his father's side, the boy let out a relieved sigh. He began to look around the fields, eager to catch sight of one of the Fair Folk.

As they moved down the hill, herding the sheep toward their farmhouse, which was just a spot in the distance, the young boy peered up at the sky and down at the ground. Spotting something green on a nearby flower, he stopped and pointed it out to his father. "Is that one of the Fair Folk?" he asked hopefully.

The shepherd shook his head. "No," he answered. "That's a grasshopper."

Pointing at another flower, the boy once again asked, "Is that one?"

Once again, the shepherd shook his head. "No, that's a dragonfly," he said. Realizing that until he gave his son more information there would be many more questions, the shepherd added, "Not all of the Fair Folk are small. Some are as big as we are. Some have wings and some don't. But they *all* have pointy ears."

Reaching up, the boy rubbed his own ears. His eyes grew wide. "Papa!" he shouted. "I think I'm one!"

Stifling a chuckle, the shepherd stopped and turned toward his son. "Let me see those ears," he said, gently examining the boy's head. "No, not pointy." Then he turned his son around. "And no wings, either. You're just a boy."

The son smiled, relieved. While he wanted to see

one of the magical creatures, he definitely did not want to *be* one.

Raising a finger, the shepherd pointed to the land that bordered their family's grazing fields. "If you *were* one of them," the boy's father went on, "you'd live in there. That's the Moors—where the faeries live. That's what all the fuss is about."

The boy's gaze followed his father's finger, and his eyes grew large. He had never seen the Moors before. Their farmhouse was too far away. But he had heard his brothers talk about sheep wandering in and never returning. Even in the warm glow of afternoon light, the Moors were covered in mist, hiding anything or anyone who walked upon them. They stretched out in both directions, with tall trees that twisted and turned toward the sky concealing the land beyond. At the base of the trunks, cattails grew tall in the dappled sunshine, stretching out toward the human land as though they were curious. The little boy shivered.

Turning his attention once more to the sheep, the shepherd resumed his walk down the hill. Behind him, the boy lingered, his eyes glued to the Moors. He could just make out food on the ground, along with totems and talismans that swung from the branches of the trees that edged the faerie land. Squinting, he tried to make out more through the mist. Unable to, and overcome with curiosity, the young boy began walking toward the misty glen.

Moments later, he found himself at the edge of the Moors, the mist clearing around him enough that he could make out the rocks and small shrubs that covered the ground. Kneeling down, he reached into his pocket and cautiously placed his half-eaten sweet cake on a rock. Impatiently, he grabbed a fistful of dirt and spattered it around the rock. He took a step back and waited.

Nothing happened.

The boy nudged the cake closer to the center of the rock.

Still nothing happened.

Disappointed, the boy turned to go. The sun would be setting at any moment, and he needed to return home with his father. Suddenly, he heard a soft fluttering sound behind him. The boy stopped. Turning back around slowly, he watched with wide eyes as a pair of small, insect-like antennae rose over the rock's edge.

Quickly, the young boy ducked behind a nearby stone, his heart racing and his breath coming in short gasps. The antennae quivered as if testing the air. A moment later, two tiny blue wings came into view, and then a brilliant blue faerie climbed onto the rock. Her skin was almost iridescent, like a dewdrop, and her colorful wings were mesmerizing as they fluttered behind her. She was the most beautiful thing the boy had ever seen.

Unaware that she had company, the tiny faerie reached out toward the sweet cake.

Behind his stone, the boy felt his nose twitch. He wiggled it, trying to prevent the inevitable. But there was nothing he could do. He sneezed.

Spinning around, the faerie locked eyes with the young boy. For a moment, neither of them moved, each in awe of the other. But then there was a loud bark and one of the collies bounded over. Before the boy could say a word, the faerie flew off, leaving the sweet cake behind.

With a sigh, the boy stood up and began to walk away from the Moors, his mind racing with thoughts and questions. What kind of faerie had that been? Was she young or old? Was she nice or mean? Were there many more like her? And most important, where was she going?

CHAPTER ONE

THE BLUE DEW FAERIE FLEW QUICKLY AWAY FROM THE YOUNG BOY WITH HIS FRIGHTENING FURRY CREATURE. AS SHE MADE HER WAY FARTHER AND FARTHER INTO THE MOORS, THE SUN SET FARTHER AND FARTHER INTO THE HORIZON, RELEASING HUES OF BRILLIANT PINKS, PURPLES, AND BLUES. The sky grew darker, and the sounds of nature became louder. There were the hoots of owls, the cawing of crows, and the buzzing drone of bugs as they went from flower to flower. Behind her, the trees that provided a natural barrier to her world faded into the distance, but bigger, older ones came into view. Their trunks ranged in color from dark brown to light gray. They rose high into the sky, creating a canopy that provided a roof of sorts for the Moors below. Within the canopy, birds called to one another while squirrels raced from branch to branch, undaunted by the height.

The faerie moved quickly along. She passed a large pond where a group of faeries splashed about, sending water droplets glittering into the air. Waving, she continued on, flying up over a hill and down through a small glen. She veered to the right at a large tree that was split in two, and made her way through a field of bright red flowers that stretched on for nearly ten tree lengths. Beyond that was another pond, this one murkier, with a dark cave at one end that was home to a family of mudgeons. She ducked her head so as not to make eye contact. The tiny creatures—with their big ears, and foreheads that were always wrinkled, as they tended to worry about everything—were sweet, but they were a bit too relaxed in their housekeeping for her taste. The dew faerie's wings beat faster and faster.

Finally, she arrived in a beautiful wooded grove, the Faerie Mound. In the very heart of the Moors, the Mound was a special place to all who lived there. Imbued with magic, the Faerie Mound practically pulsed with energy drawn from the creatures and flora that inhabited it. Naturally circular, it consisted of large peat bogs, several small streams, and, taking up the most room, a large tree that sat perched above everything. Landing on a small rock on the edge of a bog, the dew faerie looked around and smiled, happy to be home and to see so many familiar faces.

There was the grunt of a wallerbog as he sank his ungainly body into the muddy bog to join several others. The creatures all had long pointy ears that hung out from the sides of their heads and thick antennae fringed with pink. Together, they sat, their slobber dripping into the bog, creating more mud, which helped it survive.

Farther down from the bog, purple fishlike creatures with huge eyes and large mouths filtered dirty water through their netlike fins, making it fresh and clean once more. Nearby, a group of stone faeries, gray hairless creatures that looked like the rocks they worked with, kept themselves busy arranging stones in the now clean stream to help the water flow. Everywhere in the wooded grove, the creatures worked together to keep nature balanced and in harmony.

In the middle of it all sat the Rowan Tree. Enormous and stately, the tree's trunk twisted up into thick, long branches and down into a mossy maze of perfectly curled roots. Shiny leaves covered the branches, and when the moon caught them just right, they cast a green light that shone through the grove. Sitting against the sturdy trunk was a beautiful human-sized faerie, her baby cradled in one arm. The faerie's raven-colored hair shone in the moonlight, and her expansive wings gracefully rested over them both, like a feathered blanket. She hummed a lullaby and raised one hand above her, making night blossoms suddenly unfurl on the branches overhead. Then she made the leaves and flowers dance, swaying to the tune of her song, as her daughter was lulled to sleep.

"Hermia," called a warm voice behind her. Suddenly, a tall, handsome faerie appeared by her side. It was her husband, Lysander, his green eyes gleaming as brightly as the stars above them.

"Shhh," she chided gently. "She's fast asleep."

"Ah, that she is." He smiled and tilted his head, basking in the vision of his sleeping beauty. He bent down to kiss his daughter on the forehead and embrace his wife.

"How did it go?" she asked once he'd settled in next to her against the Rowan Tree.

He sighed, his brow furrowing into a frown. "It didn't. The humans did not come. I waited at the border until the sun set, and then headed back."

Hermia mulled over this information, knowing the implications of one more day lost in their efforts for peace. Though most Fair Folk distrusted all humans, having witnessed countless attacks initiated by their kind, Lysander and Hermia believed that they could not judge a whole species on the actions of a few. That peace between the races was possible. In fact, for years, they had forged relationships with local farmers and shepherds. These folks were proof that there *were* humans who appreciated nature as much as they did. In fact, the seeds for their home, the Rowan Tree, had come as a gift from one family who'd thanked them for helping with their crops after a drought. And with just a touch of their magical coaxing, they had turned the seeds into their splendid abode, a piece of nature revered by all the creatures in the Moors, despite its origins.

However, it seemed their new fragile harmony with humans, as delicate as a twig, was in danger of snapping. Sentries, the twelve-foot-tall tree-like creatures who guarded the border, had alerted the Fair Folk that humans in armor had been poking around the area, which greatly alarmed most of the other faeries. They thought this was a sure sign of a new batch of humans looking to invade and drain the Moors of its riches, the start of a new war. Hoping to break the longstanding cycle of violence, Lysander had decided to go to the border to initiate peace talks.

"What did Balthazar make of it?" Hermia asked, referencing one of the towering border guards.

"He was concerned. They have been coming to the great waterfall every day at the same time for a week. It is strange they suddenly stopped their visits."

Hermia didn't respond. The silence was thick

between them, but they each knew what was on the other's mind: The foolish hope that perhaps these humans had merely wanted to explore the Moors, or that if their mission was malicious, they had abandoned it. The fear that they had missed the opportunity to change the course of history, to create a peaceful environment in which their daughter would grow. The undeniable foreboding tension in the air.

"Tomorrow," Lysander said, breaking the silence. "I will return tomorrow."

"And I will go with you," Hermia added. "I need to be there. Maleficent will be in good hands here with the others."

A mild wind breezed through the branches. Hermia rested her head on Lysander's shoulder; he rested his head on hers. And with that, despite the heaviness in their hearts, they joined their daughter in a calm sleep under the rustling leaves of the Rowan Tree.

They heard the screeching birds first. Then the screaming.

"War! We're at war!" a stone faerie cried.

"The humans have attacked!" a water faerie yelled.

Both Hermia and Lysander jumped up, their wings unfurling instinctively. It was still nighttime, and the sky was now a starless black. Faeries and animals alike raced around on the leaf-covered land, through the burbling streams, and in the velvety air. Hermia looked down at the precious bundle in her arms. Surprisingly, the chaos had not awoken Maleficent.

Three disheveled pixies flew past them in a hurry.

"What's happened?" Hermia stood in front of them, blocking their way.

"The humans are here. At the border. A whole army of them!" one, called Knotgrass, shouted hysterically.

"With weapons!" said a pixie in blue, named Flittle.

"And ugly outfits!" added the smallest, Thistlewit.

Her eyes worried, Hermia turned to Lysander as the pixies flew away.

"There may still be time." Lysander answered her unspoken question. "If we can just reason with them . . ."

"Yes," Hermia agreed hurriedly. "We need to get to

the border." She held the sleeping infant closer to her as they flew down to the lush area directly underneath the Rowan Tree. Searching the mossy inlet, they started calling their friends' names:

"Adella? Finch? Sweetpea?"

"Robin!" Hermia cried as she saw the small, sprightly faerie buzzing toward them. Robin had been a family friend for ages. With a childlike spirit, he was always good at telling silly jokes or coming up with games, a much-needed ray of brightness and positivity during the dark times that too often plagued the Moors. That night his elf-like features formed a grave expression. It was the most serious they had ever seen him.

"There you three are! We've been looking every-where for you, we have," he announced when he reached them. "The burrow over yonder is acting as a safe haven for those not fighting. Come on, this way, if you please." He started to fly in the direction from which he'd come.

"No." Hermia stopped him. "Please, we want Maleficent to go with you to the safe haven, but we will not."

"We're heading to the front lines," Lysander explained.

Robin looked at them for a moment. Then he nodded. He knew about their longstanding efforts to initiate peace—and how much it would mean to them to stop the fighting for good. Arguing with them would only waste time.

"All right, then," he replied. "But follow me to the burrow on your way there. Don't think I could hold her meself."

The faeries flew single file, silent amid the loud disorder around them. Only when Maleficent was kissed by her parents, gently placed inside the cozy burrow, and surrounded by a mélange of colorful creatures cooing over her did any of them speak.

"Thank you," Lysander said to Robin meaningfully. "We'll be back as soon as we can."

Then he and Hermia swiftly took off into the black night once more, heading toward the loud noises and flashing lights at the border, until they looked like small ravens soaring in the sky.

As soon as they were out of sight, Robin turned to look at the resting baby, her lips slightly parted, her stomach moving with sleepy waves of breath. She did not know her parents had just flown off into danger so that the Moors could thrive once more.

"Keep sleeping, love," he whispered to her. "We'll look after you."

CHAPTER TWO

AS DID MOST NIGHTS FILLED WITH UNWANTED EXCITEMENT, THE EVENING DRAGGED ON SLOWLY. THE FAERIES IN THE BURROW DIDN'T THINK THEY WOULD BE ABLE TO SLEEP THROUGH THE TERRIFYING SOUNDS. Nor did they think the sun would ever rise again to create another morning. But sleep the faeries did, and up the sun rose, marking the start of a new dawn . . . and a new age. The sun brought with it a chorus of singing birds and a flurry of activity throughout the Moors.

"It's over!" shouted a hedgehog faerie nearby.

"It's over!" echoed a few dew faeries flying overhead.

Robin awoke with a start. He furtively looked around. He was alone in the dark burrow. If it had been any other day, he would have laughed merrily, thinking he'd been roped into a game of hide-and-go-seek. Instead, he panicked.

"Maleficent! Pompous possums, where could she have . . . where could they have . . . Maleficent!" he squeaked as he raced out of the burrow.

"It's all right." It was a voice as bright as tinkling bells, his friend Sweetpea's voice.

Robin turned to his right and saw baby Maleficent lying in a large nest next to a shallow stream. Four energetic water faeries, Crisith, Lockstone, Walla, and Pipsy, were cleaning her soft black hair, dropping small amounts of the clear sparkling water over her head. Maleficent shifted in the nest, reaching toward them, while Sweetpea and Finch decorated the nest with leaves and flowers.

"They have been spreading the news all morning," Sweetpea announced. "The battle is over. The Moors are safe once more."

"We want to get Maleficent ready to see Hermia and Lysander when they get back. I'm sure they'll be here any moment," Finch added, hovering back to observe their masterpiece. He then made his way back to adjust a leaf that was out of place.

Robin broke into a smile and then erupted into laughter. "Whooping wallerbogs! They did it!" He buzzed over to Maleficent and tickled her cheeks. She giggled and clapped her hands in delight.

A few hours later, after the fruit faerie Adella had fed Maleficent some berries and Robin had played a few dozen rounds of peekaboo with her, Maleficent started to cry quietly. Robin didn't know if she was in tune with their shared feelings of uneasiness, or if she intuitively knew something was wrong. But his suspicions were confirmed when he saw a giant sentry slowly headed their way.

The towering wooden creatures hardly ever came to that part of the Moors. They were far more comfortable in the marsh and took their duties as guards of the border seriously. Only something truly important would have brought him there, particularly after a battle. As the sentry ambled on, his large footsteps echoing and his grand shadow sweeping past, many other creatures and Fair Folk came out of the surrounding area to gather together.

"What brings you here, Birchalin?" asked Robin when he approached the group. "When can we expect Lysander and Hermia?"

The sentry sighed, shifting his weight from root to root. "I'm afraid I come bearing bad news. I wanted to be the one to deliver it, but now it is so hard to say."

Some of the faeries flew up to his height and gathered round the wooden creature to hear him. They were at once anxious to listen and afraid of what he might say.

"I thought we won the battle," Finch offered.

"We did keep our home safe from the humans once more, for the time being," Birchalin began softly. "But I'm afraid our victory came at a price. Lysander and Hermia were killed last night."

A chorus of gasps shuddered through the crowd,

and Maleficent started to wail louder in her nest on the ground. The other Fair Folk looked at her, a wave of shock and sorrow for the infant faerie passing through them all.

Robin was the one to move first. Slowly, but with purpose, he flew down to Maleficent's side, touching her shoulder with a small hand. One by one, others followed suit, Sweetpea and Finch at her feet, the water faeries by her head, wallerbogs rising out of their lake to sit by her side.

Then they lifted her into the air, flying through the forest with Birchalin and other creatures following, creating a somber procession. Finally, they reached their destination, the place to which they had all known they were going without having to say it aloud. The Rowan Tree. Gently, they lowered Maleficent against the magnificent stump, beams of sunlight peeking through the leaves, creating a halo around her head. As she settled into the tree, she stopped crying.

The other Fair Folk stood and flew around her,

forming a protective circle. Robin was the first to speak, repeating the words he'd spoken only hours earlier.

"We'll look after you."

As the years passed, Maleficent grew to be a striking, happy faerie child. The Fair Folk raised her together, taking care of her, teaching her all of their skills, their languages, their work, until it was apparent she no longer needed looking after. She was a quick learner and proved to be lively and independent at a very young age. Soon the other Fair Folk became her dearest companions and friends instead of her caretakers, and she made sure to visit them all throughout the day. Her favorite visits were the ones during which the others would tell her about her parents.

"Oh, you have your mother's wings," Sweetpea would say during a morning flight. Maleficent flew haphazardly next to her, unable to control her large, ungainly wings just yet. But hearing that her oversized ebony wings were similar to her mother's made Maleficent blush proudly.

"Your dad had those same glittering eyes," Finch

would remark as they walked through the forest. She looked at herself in the gleaming pond, paying closer attention to her bright eyes.

Maleficent most enjoyed spending time with her best friend, Robin. Sometimes they'd play made-up games, trying to get each other to guess what animals they were pretending to be, or rewarding whomever made the strangest-looking face that day. Often he'd teach her how to play funny little tricks on the nearby faeries. Their shoulders would shake with laughter when they saw the bewilderment on the stone faerie's face after they moved her recently arranged rocks right next to her. Or when the pixies bickered with one another, not knowing that Robin and Maleficent were the ones who had eaten their berries.

Other times, they would sit lazily in the Rowan Tree. He had known her parents the best and told her stories about them all the time. Sometimes they were silly, sometimes they were sweet, but they always made her smile.

"And then I popped up from under the bog, scaring

the living fireflies out of Lysander, I did." Robin guffawed, thinking of the memory, and Maleficent joined in.

"Oh, Robin, you devil! When he was trying so hard to impress my mother," she said, giggling.

"He still impressed her, even after jumping ten feet high like a scared ninny."

After their laughter subsided, Maleficent broached the subject that Robin so carefully avoided.

"Robin . . . have you ever seen a human close-up?"

He frowned. "No, lass, I have not. Nor would I want to. They're nothing but trouble, humans."

Maleficent sat up, talking more animatedly now. "But you said my parents believed there were good ones out there. That we could have a good relationship with them someday."

"I did," Robin agreed. "But you know what that belief cost them." He spoke gently but firmly. It was sometimes hard to remember how young, how innocent Maleficent still was. "They try to steal our treasures, pillage our land. They even carry weapons made out of iron, they do, the stuff that burns our kind."

"But, Robin, humans are a part of nature, too," she continued. She'd clearly been thinking quite a bit about this. "I know there are horrendous ones. Monsters. But there are mean faeries and animals out there, too, just like there are plenty of nice ones. The humans cannot be all bad."

Robin sat quietly. He could not give her the answer she wanted. After that dreadful night years earlier, he despised all humans for what they'd taken away. "No, my love," he said, patting her arm. "They are." He flew away from the Rowan Tree, unable to continue their conversation.

Maleficent sighed, resting her back against the trunk of the tree once more. Maybe Robin didn't believe it, but she did. And she knew her parents would be proud of her for doing so.

CHAPTER THREE

TWO YEARS HAD PASSED, YET THE ROWAN TREE REMAINED MOSTLY THE SAME, ITS TWISTED TRUNK ONLY SLIGHTLY DARKER WITH AGE AND ITS BRANCHES ONLY A LITTLE MORE BOWED. WHILE THE TREE HAD NOT CHANGED MUCH, ITS INHABITANT HAD.

Unfolding her wings, Maleficent lifted herself up and out of the Rowan Tree. As her wings carried her higher into the sky, she soared on the wind, dipping and spinning with ease over the Moors. Gone were the awkward days when she had no control. Now Maleficent and her wings were one. Climbing higher and higher into the sky, she burst through the clouds and then hung suspended in the air. A look of pure joy washed over her face as she delighted in the moment. Then, with a laugh, she swooped back down.

She flew along a rushing river, the water burbling happily over boulders of various sizes. As she saw the rocks, a glimmer came into Maleficent's eyes and she began to gesture with her hands. Below, the boulders began to move and shift according to Maleficent's magical direction. When she was done, she paused to look over her handiwork—a beautiful waterfall.

That task complete, she continued along, greeting the river rock creatures as she passed them. "Morning!"

She flew over the wallerbogs, who were jovially throwing mud at one another. As soon as they noticed her, one of them wound up, ready to include Maleficent in their game.

"No, no, don't do it!" Maleficent warned. "Don't you—"

The wallerbog threw the mud, missing Maleficent and hitting a hedgehog faerie instead.

"Ha! You missed me!" Maleficent laughed, waving good-bye and flying through the forest above a few skating water fairies.

"Lovely work, girls," she called. She looked behind

her to see some pesky dew faeries following her. "Hey! Find your own gusts of wind!"

Suddenly, Maleficent noticed Knotgrass, Flittle, and Thistlewit waving at her from a rock. The three pixies could be rather vain and flighty, but they'd never looked so agitated.

"What's all the fuss?" she asked, landing in front of them.

Knotgrass started speaking rapidly. "Maleficent, did you hear? The border guards have—"

"Why do you get to tell her?" Flittle interrupted her. "I want to tell her!"

"I want to!" Thistlewit echoed.

Maleficent shifted, growing weary of their tiresome ways. "Tell me what?"

"Maleficent, the border guards . . ." Flittle started.

"The border guards have found a human thief at the pool of jewels!" Thistlewit burst out. "Sorry," she said to the other pixies.

Maleficent's eyes grew wide and she took off into the air, hundreds of thoughts reeling in her head. A human. Here in the Moors. Of course, Robin would never approve of her going to meet it. But now was her chance to see what a human was like. Maleficent's curiosity was piqued.

Maleficent landed on a rock in front of the great waterfall. The two guarding sentries stood in the water, gesturing toward a part of the brush. Seeing Maleficent, Balthazar called out to her in his native woodish tongue.

"I'm not afraid," Maleficent told him. "Besides, I've never seen a human up close." She peered through the brush and made out the figure of a boy about her age.

"What did he take from the pool?" she asked.

Balthazar screeched, answering her.

A stone. She sighed. "Come out!" she said to the brush.

"No!" came a defiant voice from behind it. "They mean to kill me. And besides, they're hideous to look at."

Balthazar screeched once more, this time quite offended.

"That's extremely rude!" Maleficent chided. To

Balthazar she said, "Don't listen to him. You're classi-cally handsome." She turned once more to the brush, her patience wearing thin. "It's not right to steal but we don't kill people for it. Come out. Come out this instant!"

A slight boy dressed in meager clothes emerged. His eyes widened at the sight of Maleficent.

"You're her," he said.

Maleficent looked him up and down. He was about her height, which seemed small for a human. "Are you fully grown?"

"No."

Maleficent turned to Balthazar. "I believe he's just a boy."

"And you're just a girl," the boy said. "I think."

Maleficent narrowed her eyes. "Who are you?"

"I'm called Stefan. Who are you?"

"I'm Maleficent." She paused and then asked the question she really wanted to ask. "Do you intend us harm?"

Stefan blinked at her, clearly surprised. "What? No."

"Then I'll guide you out of the Moors."

Balthazar screeched once more.

"Yes, right," she answered. She looked at Stefan. "You have to give it back."

"Give what back?" Stefan asked.

Maleficent shared a look with the sentries and sighed. Holding out her hand, she stared at Stefan, who groaned, knowing he'd been beat. He reached into his pocket, pulled out a beautiful stone, and tossed it to her. Maleficent caught it smoothly, and gently tossed it into the glittering water. Then she gestured for Stefan to follow her. She felt bad for the human. Since he didn't have wings, they'd have to go on foot.

"If I knew you would throw it away, I would have kept it," Stefan whined.

"I didn't throw it away. I delivered it home. As I'm going to do for you."

They walked in silence for a while, Maleficent guiding Stefan through the forest and into a clearing. In the distance, past acres of fields, stood the castle. Maleficent stared at it, wondering what would be so appealing about closing oneself off from the outside with such high walls.

Noticing Maleficent's gaze, Stefan said, "Someday I'll live there. In the castle."

Maleficent was not impressed. "Where do you live now?"

"In a barn," Stefan replied.

Now this was something Maleficent wanted to hear more about. "A barn? So your parents are farmers, then?"

"My parents are dead."

Maleficent looked at Stefan sharply. Maybe they had more in common than she'd thought. "Mine too," she said softly.

"How did they die, plague?" Stefan asked.

"They were killed by humans. In the last war." She gestured toward the forest. "Now all the family I have is in there."

Stefan frowned. "That's sad."

"No it's not," Maleficent responded defensively. "They're all I need."

"We'll see each other again," Stefan said suddenly.

Maleficent sighed, knowing how much Robin and the other Fair Folk distrusted humans. "You really shouldn't come back here, you know. It's not safe."

"Would that not be up to me?" Stefan asked, stepping toward her.

"It would," she replied.

"And if I made that choice, if I came back . . . would you be here?" He was only a few inches away from her now.

Maleficent suddenly felt awkward and nervous. "Perhaps."

He offered his hand, and she reached out to take it. Suddenly, a searing hot flash hit her finger, and she pulled her hand back. Glancing down, she saw his ring had left a red burn.

"What happened?" Stefan asked, shocked.

"Your ring is made of iron," Maleficent explained, shaking her hand to alleviate the pain.

"I'm sorry." Then he took the ring off and tossed it far into the field. Maleficent was touched. No one had ever done something so selfless for her.

Stefan smiled and turned to walk away. She watched him hurry down a hill and then turn around.

"I like your wings!" he called.

Maleficent smiled widely, which turned into a giggle despite her. It appeared her parents had been right. Not all humans were bad. Though she felt she'd better keep this rendezvous a secret from the others for now. She knew they would just tell her how dangerous it was to talk to a human.

At a distance, Stefan ran his fingers over the other smooth stone he had taken from the pool, which lay safely in his pocket.

CHAPTER FOUR

A WEEK LATER, MALEFICENT FLEW HIGH IN THE AIR, NOTICING A FAMILIAR FIGURE ROAMING AROUND THE FOREST CLEARING.

SHE SMILED AND ACCELERATED, THEN GENTLY DROPPED DOWN BEHIND STEFAN. He turned, startled by her sudden appearance.

"Well, well. Look who came back," she said.

"I thought it was worth the risk."

Maleficent blushed as a small deer emerged from a stand of trees.

"If I had my bow, I'd make you a fine dinner," Stefan said, gesturing toward the animal.

Choosing to ignore the remark, Maleficent walked over to the deer. It was a beautiful creature. She held out her hand in a greeting and kneeled before it. The deer nuzzled against her palm.

"Magic," Stefan breathed, watching them.

"No. Just kindness," Maleficent said, correcting him. She kept her gaze on the deer.

Stefan headed behind her, prompting the deer to walk away. Rising, Maleficent turned to face him.

"When we met, you said, 'You're her.' What did you mean?" she asked.

"People have seen you. Flying. The girl from the Moors that looks just like us . . . except for your wings." He stared at them, clearly wanting to take a closer look. Maleficent held out a wing toward him.

"You sure?" he asked.

She nodded, and he gently touched the wing. "They're beautiful."

"Thank you," Maleficent said, looking over her shoulder. "They are special, aren't they?"

Next Stefan looked up at Maleficent's horns. "Are they sharp?" he asked.

The faerie felt her face turn red, and she bowed her head, suddenly feeling self-conscious.

"They're majestic," Stefan continued. "That's the

word. They are far and away the most majestic horns that I have ever seen."

Maleficent was overcome with emotion. Without thinking, she hugged him. His body stiffened; it was clear he hadn't been expecting this reaction. But soon she felt him smile.

"We can choose to be friends," Maleficent said. "Why can't the others?"

"Maybe they can. Maybe we can show them."

So Maleficent and Stefan bonded over a hope for peace, something that made Maleficent feel closer to her parents than ever. Stefan came to the edge of the Moors, the place that became their secret spot. They talked about their lives, their future. Then, on Maleficent's sixteenth birthday, they kissed—a kiss so pure, so honest, so real that it was True Love's Kiss.

But as the years marched on, Stefan spent less time visiting the Moors and Maleficent. He was busy making good on his promise to live in the castle, albeit as a servant. He seemed less concerned with building harmony between the humans and faeries, and more concerned with his life at the castle—a life he seemed to want to keep private. No matter what questions Maleficent asked out of genuine interest, Stefan avoided answering them.

One day, Maleficent soared in the sky, spotting Stefan nearby on a cliff. It had been weeks since she'd last seen him.

"Stefan," she called down to him.

"Hello," he replied.

"Hello," Maleficent repeated. She suddenly felt awkward around him.

"Where have you been?" Stefan asked.

Maleficent narrowed her eyes. "I've been looking for you."

"Really?"

"Yes," she responded. "You're always disappearing these days." She lowered herself to him for a kiss. They leaned close together. And for a fleeting moment, it all felt right again.

CHAPTER FIVE

MALEFICENT LEANED AGAINST THE ROWAN TREE, WATCHING THE END OF ANOTHER DAY. IT HAD BEEN A MONTH SINCE SHE'D SEEN STEFAN, THE LONGEST TIME YET. ROBIN AND THE OTHER FAIR FOLK HAD NOTICED HER GROWING MORE SOLEMN AND QUIET, BUT SHE WAS TOO ASHAMED TO ADMIT SHE WAS FEELING A LITTLE LOVESICK, PARTICULARLY FOR A HUMAN BOY. She distanced herself from them, preferring to be alone in case she grew tempted to tell them about her companion, or in case Stefan suddenly appeared.

As the sun set, Maleficent's thoughts grew dark as well. She wondered where Stefan was. If he was okay. If he missed her, even a little. Try as she might, Maleficent couldn't shake the sadness that filled her. Was she wrong to trust a human? Had her parents been wrong, too? Not for the first time, she wondered what things would have been like had her parents lived. She could just picture the scene—running home to the Rowan Tree and finding her mother sitting there, her back against the warm trunk. Maleficent would cry and tell her everything, and then her mother would kiss her forehead and tell her it would be all right. And it would be. Somehow.

Maleficent shook her head. It was silly to get caught up in a fantasy. She sighed and gave herself a mental shake. She had to snap out of her melancholy. Perhaps she would see what Robin was up to after all. He was always good at cheering her up.

Suddenly, there was a sound like thunder. Looking over the precipice, Maleficent let out a gasp. She had been so caught up in her thoughts that she hadn't noticed the approaching army. It was charging toward the Moors, King Henry's banner flying in the wind. Her heart sank in her chest. It was happening again. Another war. Quickly, Maleficent took to the sky.

• • •

In the countryside at the edge of the Moors, King Henry sat on his horse, addressing his army. Henry was a man long past his prime. His beard was gray and the wavy hair on his head was thinning. His waist had thickened over the years and his fingers ached with arthritis. Despite all that, he held himself proudly, comfortable in his heavy armor. This was not the first time he had gone to war. A kingdom was only as strong as the king who sat on its throne, and Henry had, on more occasions than he could count, proven his strength.

But that day was different. More was at stake than ever before. The land in the Moors was vast and, from all reports, full of riches beyond imagining. There were natural resources, such as fresh water and plentiful forests. And it was rumored that the streams were filled with jewels. Taking over the Moors would make his kingdom much more powerful.

But those were not reasons why Henry now stood in front of his army at the edge of the Moors. The reason Henry was about to go to war was that the Moors posed a huge threat. The creatures who lived there had magic.

And there was no telling what they might someday do with that magic. So Henry wanted them destroyed. And if a consequence of that destruction was access to rich lands, all the better.

As his mount pranced nervously under him, Henry gestured behind himself. "There they are," he began. "The mysterious Moors. No one dares to venture there for fear of the magical creatures that lurk within." He paused, scanning the crowd for the telltale signs of weakness and fright. Seeing only a handful of men who looked ready to turn back, he went on. "Well, I say . . . crush them!"

The army let out a loud cheer. Emboldened, King Henry lengthened his pep talk. "We're not afraid of 'magical' creatures!" he cried. "We have swords!" The men waved their weapons high in the air and let out another cheer. "We will take the Moors and kill anything that stands in our way!"

He threw the signal and the men charged forward. The first men reached the bottom of a hill covered in mist. They began to climb, the ground shaking under their pounding footsteps. And then they came to a screeching halt.

From the other side of the hill, two enormous black wings appeared through the mist. Then a pair of sharp, twisted horns. Slowly, Maleficent rose into the air, looking like a creature from hell. Behind her, there was only mist. No army of her own. No faeries or creatures. Just Maleficent.

For a moment, Henry was worried. He had been prepared to take the Moors unawares. And the creature hovering in front of them *was* rather scary. But then he smiled. There appeared to be only one.

"Go no further," Maleficent instructed, sounding braver than she felt.

King Henry smirked at her gall. "A king does not take orders from a winged elf."

"You are no king to me."

Henry yelled to his troops, "Bring me her head!"

Once more, the army thundered forward, the sound of hoofbeats mixing with the clinking of armor. As Maleficent watched them approach, her heart thudded in her chest. She couldn't help thinking this was what her parents must have seen and felt during their final moments. But she would do anything to protect the Moors, just as they had. Lifting her wings higher, she let out an ear-piercing shriek and began to fly forward.

And then, from behind her, she felt a surge of magic. Turning, she watched as a malevolent army appeared. They clawed and climbed their way up the hill. Some of the creatures were scaled, others had feet turned backward, while others had leather wings. Some snarled, while others slobbered like diseased hounds. There were ones who walked upright and others who crawled along on four legs. But they all had one thing in common: they wanted to protect their home. And they had defended this place from invading humans many times before.

As the hodgepodge army of creatures approached, Maleficent nearly cried in relief. She had been so scared that she wouldn't be able to rise to the occasion to fight at the front lines if it had ever come to this. But now she had her army, who had no doubt rushed to her aid when they had learned of the trouble, and she felt braver with the creatures behind her. She had become their make-shift leader. And they were ready. Giving a signal, she watched as they began to attack viciously.

Confident that the creatures could take care of the larger army, Maleficent set her sights on King Henry. As soon as he had seen the Moorland army, the king had turned his horse and begun racing for home. But Maleficent wasn't going to let him go that easily. He was one of the monstrous humans. The kind Robin had warned her about. The kind who came to destroy every-thing she cared about for his own gain. The kind who had killed her parents. Her fury rising as she took to the air, she flew after him.

It took her only a moment to catch up to Henry. From above, she battered the king with her wings until he fell off his horse. She landed and stood looming above him. "You will not have the Moors now or ever!" she cried, her voice booming.

Frightened, King Henry raised his armored hand, trying to protect himself from Maleficent. As he did, the iron gently brushed Maleficent's cheek.

She let out a gasp and raised a hand to her face. Where the iron had touched her skin, it burned painfully.

Noticing that his enemy was distracted, King Henry scrambled to his feet and hobbled away, wheezing in pain. All around him, the rest of the army retreated as well, running as fast as they could from the terrifying creatures.

Sighing, Maleficent gave a signal, and her army ceased its attack. Maleficent saw more familiar faces among the ranks. Balthazar nodded at Maleficent and she nodded back, hoping she was conveying the gratitude she felt. Robin, though shaken, looked undeniably proud of her. She bowed her head and flew away, afraid that if he looked at her long enough, he could tell she'd been spending time with one of the humans he despised, even if the human seemed to be good.

As she headed back into the Moors, Maleficent was left alone with her thoughts. A human attack. Could they dare to hope that this would be the end of it? That peace could still be possible? How she wished she could talk to Stefan. Maybe they could make a plan to form some sort of treaty between the faeries and the humans. But a nagging notion interrupted her other thoughts: what if Robin was right? What if all the humans banded together against them? What if Stefan sided with King Henry?

CHAPTER SIX

KING HENRY LAY IN BED, DOZENS OF COUNCILMEN AND GENERALS SURROUNDING HIM. FROM AN ALCOVE, STEFAN WATCHED THE SCENE, LIGHTING THE LAST CANDELABRA. HE HAD TO LEAN IN CLOSELY TO HEAR WHAT THE WEAKENED KING WAS SAYING.

"When I took the throne, I promised the people that one day we would take the Moors and their treasures. And each of you swore allegiance to me and to that cause." He started coughing violently, sputtering as he tried to sit up. Stefan appeared with a pillow and placed it behind the king's back.

"Defeated in battle," the king continued as if there had been no interruption. "Is this to be my legacy? I see you waiting for me to die. You won't have long to wait. But what then? Who will rule? My daughter? Or perhaps I will choose my successor."

An audible intake of breath sounded from the other men. One of them, be king? They all stood a bit straighter.

"But who among you is worthy?" The king's eyes flashed with anger. "Kill her! Kill the faerie, and avenge me. Upon my death you will take the crown!"

Stefan backed away from the bed quietly, knowing that as a servant, he would not be missed. Once he stood outside the king's chamber, he panted, his palms against his knees. He knew what he had to do.

"Maleficent? Maleficent?" Stefan called out. It had been so long since he'd set foot in their old secret spot, but it was as beautiful and serene as it always had been.

Maleficent landed swiftly behind him. He spun around, surprised. He almost laughed, thinking how he should have been used to her entrances by then.

She eyed him wordlessly for a moment, trying to see if he had changed. It was as though he had never left. He still wore his threadbare clothes and a flask at his side. But Maleficent was even stronger now after winning a battle, aware of her power and authority, her ability to protect her friends and her home. She had been reminded of the Moors' war-stricken past, why the others were so suspicious of outsiders.

At the same time, she couldn't help feeling a flutter in her stomach as she looked upon his familiar and comforting face. Forcing the sensation aside, she squared her shoulders and raised one perfectly arched eyebrow. "How is life with the humans?" she asked.

He stared at the ground, clearly uncomfortable. "They are horrible," he said after a moment. "And they will not stop. They mean to kill you." He looked up into her eyes.

Maleficent listened carefully. She had once loved this human deeply. Now she wasn't sure if she could trust Stefan.

"When we first met, you told me never to come here again. But I did, and I told you it was worth the risk." He brushed her hair out of her face. "It still is. I have chosen."

Stepping closer to her, he whispered, "I belong here, with you. If you'll have me."

Maleficent relaxed, moved by his words. She hugged him as she had done the day they had first met, and it felt like everything was right once more.

A short while later, Maleficent lay snuggled in Stefan's arms. Her wings were wrapped around them like a warm blanket, and as dusk faded into the darkness of night, they continued to laugh and talk. It was a joyous occasion. She loved and was loved in return, by a human no less. Her parents' goal of peace between the races had been achieved by her. And now she and Stefan could live in the Moors together. Now there was hope for peace for everyone. She couldn't wait to introduce him to Robin and the others. It would likely take some getting used to, but in time, they would learn that an alliance with some humans was possible and could even help protect the Moors from future attacks.

Smiling to herself, she reached over and took a small drink from Stefan's flask. Then, closing her eyes, she began to drift off. The last thought she had before sleep overcame her was that maybe, just maybe, she would get to live happily ever after.

CHAPTER SEVEN

AT DAWN MALEFICENT AWOKE TO A SEARING PAIN IN HER BACK. GROANING, SHE SHOOK HER HEAD. SHE FELT GROGGY AND FUZZY, AND SHE SHOOK IT ONCE MORE, TRYING TO MAKE THE ODD FEELING DISAPPEAR. But as her head cleared, the pain returned twofold. Looking at where Stefan had been, she saw that he was gone. And then, reaching over her shoulders, she found that her wings were gone, too. All that remained was a long, thin cauterized wound where they used to be. On the ground nearby lay an iron chain, a few black feathers stuck to the links.

Shock and horror filled Maleficent as she realized what had happened. That she had been betrayed. That Stefan had taken her wings. That he had lied. Stolen her heart and her wings. As grief overtook her, she let out an anguished cry. *Why?* she screamed silently. *Why would he do this to me?* Dropping her head into her hands, she began to sob. For she knew the answer. She had known it deep inside all along. Stefan loved his world, loved his kind, more than he could ever love her. He had taken her wings to prove to that wretched King Henry that he was loyal, even though it meant being disloyal to her.

How had she been so blind? Humans had killed her parents. Humans had attacked her home time and time again. A human had ruined her chance at a happy life. She should have listened to Robin. Humans were not to be trusted. She had led them here by befriending one, and now she was paying the price. She didn't deserve to live here with the others.

In that moment, a part of her died. The part that believed in joy, hope, and peace. The part of her that believed in love. That part was gone forever. Stefan had seen to that.

"I have avenged you, sire," Stefan announced over a wheezing King Henry. Stefan was happy he wasn't too late. Pulling open his sack, he revealed Maleficent's flapping wings. Henry stared up at him, amazed.

"She is vanquished. You have done well, son," he murmured. "You have done what others feared to do. You will be rewarded."

Stefan beamed. He'd finally done it. He'd overcome his status as a poor orphan to become something great. "I shall do my best to be a worthy successor, Your Majesty."

"Successor? You?" Henry gaped at him in surprise.

"As by your edict."

The king allowed himself a throaty laugh. "You? Your blood is not worthy. You are a servant, nothing more. I don't even know your name!"

The king continued to laugh heartily, which became a series of coughs.

Stefan turned, unable to believe what he was hearing. He had not done the unthinkable to be turned away now. He walked swiftly to the other side of the bed and stood over the king. Enraged, Stefan picked up a pillow and forced it over the king's head.

"I'm called Stefan."

CHAPTER EIGHT

LYING BY THE RIVERBANK THAT ONLY AN EVENING BEFORE HAD SEEMED SO BEAUTIFUL, MALEFICENT LET DARKNESS TAKE HOLD OF HER HEART. SHE LAY THERE FOR HOURS, OCCASIONALLY FEELING THE FLAPPING OF PHANTOM WINGS. She wanted to stay there until her heart stopped. There was nothing left for her in this cruel world. So she closed her eyes and waited for the end.

But the end didn't come. For as night fell once more, Maleficent slowly awoke, aware of the sounds of nature all around her. Keeping her eyes closed, she heard the trees rustling overhead and groaned. But the trees just rustled louder, as though trying to rouse her. Their branches began to thrash angrily and the wood creaked and groaned.

Opening her eyes, Maleficent watched the trees shake. She knew they were trying to help, but she didn't care. Reaching into her robe, she pulled out a broken, crooked branch of the Rowan, a piece of home that she often carried with her. With a sigh, she let it fall to the ground.

To her surprise, the branch began to straighten out. Then it began to grow. It grew longer and thicker until it was the size of a staff. As Maleficent picked it up, her fingers wrapped tightly around it. She felt a surge of power, and despite her misery, she began to pull herself up. When she was standing, she leaned on the staff. It was hardy and bore her weight well.

Interesting, she thought as she began to limp forward. With each step, her resolve grew. True, Stefan had taken her wings. True, he had broken her heart. But she still had her magic. And now she had something stronger than magic. She had a mission. She was going to make Stefan and the humans pay for what they had done.

• • •

Maleficent wandered the countryside, and wherever she went, destruction and chaos followed. When she passed by a shepherd's paddock, the gate magically swung open and the flock of sheep ran out and scattered in all directions, their bleats slowly fading away as they disappeared into the nearby woods. The sky grew darker and the clouds thundered. As she walked through the middle of a farmer's field, the scarecrow rotted and the wheels on a nearby cart fell off. Moving down the road, she raised her staff high. The ground shook and then broke apart, rocks and debris flying high in the air. Pointing at a mound of hay in the distance, she smiled maliciously as it caught on fire and began to burn, the flames licking the sky.

With each step Maleficent grew stronger, and with each act of destruction she grew more intense, her focus fiercer. She leaned less and less on the staff until, finally, she didn't need it at all. Still, she kept it in her hand, unwilling to let go of the last part of her old life.

After a few weeks of wandering aimlessly, Maleficent

found herself outside the ruins of a long-abandoned castle. Birds' nests had replaced the panes of glass in its many windows. Whole sides of the massive building had fallen down, and only a few of the outbuildings still had roofs. Moss had overtaken the stone floors and walls, giving the whole place a green, muted atmosphere, and where horses had once munched hay in stalls, nothing remained but a few empty, rotting buckets. But as she made her way amid the broken stone and around the fallen timber, Maleficent felt at peace. This place was like her. Left to rot and ruin. And like her, it held on despite being broken. Lying down on the grass that had grown in the middle of the ruins, Maleficent looked up at the stone gargoyles perched on the roof. They glared back at her, their mouths frozen in grimaces that Maleficent found oddly comforting.

Hearing the rustle of wings, Maleficent watched as a large raven flew into the castle. The bird was carrying a piece of corn in his beak. Landing on the ground, the bird dropped the corn and then began to preen, clearly proud of his prize. As the creature pecked at the corn, Maleficent watched him sadly. The black bird's wings reminded her of the ones she had lost, and she wished, not for the first time, that she had never allowed them to be taken.

As the bird flew off, Maleficent sighed and got to her feet. It was no good to wish for things that could never happen. She had done that before and it had only ended up hurting her. She had to focus on the real things that could be done. Like making this abandoned castle her home.

For the next few days, Maleficent kept busy at the castle. There was not much she could do to rebuild, but she could at least try to make parts of it livable. And it wasn't like she needed a lot. Just a place to stay dry and hidden from any snooping humans. Having grown thirsty from her efforts, she made her way to a nearby stream. But as she bent over to drink, she heard the frightened cry of a bird from somewhere nearby. Quietly she made her way to the high reeds that lined the stream, and looked through them, kneeling down to keep herself out of sight.

On the other side, she saw the raven that had visited the ruins trapped under a thick net. Two farmers were approaching, clubs in their hands and dogs at their sides. The dogs growled at the raven, causing the creature to flap his wings frantically. But there was nowhere for him to go.

Feeling the familiar rage toward the cruel humans building up inside her, Maleficent waved her hand. "Into a man," she said.

There was a shimmer of magic, and before the shocked farmers' eyes, the raven transformed into a man. Throwing off the net, the raven-man climbed to his feet unsteadily.

"It's a demon!" one of the farmers cried. The two men turned and took off, the dogs following close behind.

When she was sure they were gone, Maleficent stood up. Her gaze fell on the bird she had transformed. As a human he was tall, with silky black hair and dark eyes that darted around nervously. While man wasn't her first choice of form, at least she had saved the creature.

Catching sight of the faerie, the raven-man cocked his head. "What have you done to me?" he asked, gesturing at his body, clearly unhappy with its present form. His voice was surprisingly rich and melodic for one not used to having the power of speech.

"Would you rather I let them beat you to death?" Maleficent asked.

The raven-man lifted his wingless arms into the air. "I'm not certain," he replied.

"Stop complaining," Maleficent said as she began to walk around him slowly, scrutinizing. She had to admit he wasn't terrible to look at, even for a human. She could have created far worse. "I saved your life."

Uncomfortable with her penetrating stare, the raven-man shifted on his feet. "Forgive me," he said.

Maleficent nodded. "What do I call you?"

"Diaval," he answered. "And in return for my life, I am your servant. Whatever you need."

Whatever I need? Maleficent mused. Well, that was certainly an interesting twist. There were so many things she did need and so much she could use. Then a smile slowly spread across her face. There *was* one thing she needed more than anything. "Wings," she said, nodding. "You'll be my wings."

CHAPTER NINE

STEFAN OBSERVED HIS SURROUNDINGS AS HE SAT PERCHED ON HIS NEW THRONE. THE ORNATE ROOM WAS THE PICTURE OF ROYALTY WITH ITS DETAILED MOLDINGS, ITS DRAPING TAPESTRIES, ITS LOFTY CEILINGS. Though he was there to be crowned the new king, he couldn't help feeling uneasy, as if the small group of advisors, the raven perched outside the window, and even the throne room itself were judging him and knew he didn't rightfully belong there.

He felt a small hand on his and looked at his new wife, Leila, sitting next to him. She was lovely. Her kind doe-like eyes met his, and he was instantly reminded of that afternoon in the Moors long before, when Maleficent had tamed the small deer with kindness, so at ease with the natural beauty around her. Leila looked nothing like Maleficent, her locks golden and curled, not ebony and straight, her eyes warm and blue instead of a piercing green. Yet he sensed the same kindness and willingness to trust within her that he'd first seen in Maleficent.

A fresh wave of guilt rose in his throat, and he pushed it down, forcing himself to concentrate on the task at hand. He'd only done what had been necessary, for his future and hers. Another man seeking the crown would have killed her. Besides, it was finished now. There was no use replaying the events in his mind. This was the moment he'd been waiting for his entire life. He was not going to let anything ruin it.

The heavy crown was finally placed on his head. He smiled. Then he cleared his throat.

"King Henry shall be missed," Stefan announced to the group of advisors before him. "And I am humbled that his final proclamation gave me this crown, this throne."

Two advisors grumbled and shared a meaningful look. Stefan felt heat suddenly rise to his face.

"What do you have to say?" he bellowed.

The advisors grew quiet, looking at Stefan nervously.

"Do you doubt me?" Stefan continued, holding up the proclamation that named him Henry's successor. He'd brought it with him just in case there was trouble. King Henry's seal gleamed in the sunlit room.

"By his own hand. Because I avenged him." He said it so righteously he almost believed that Henry had actually named him as his successor and sealed the proclamation. Really, Stefan had done it himself in Henry's chamber, shortly after the king had stopped struggling against his pillow. Stefan had lifted Henry's lifeless hand and pressed the ring onto the molten wax, ensuring his future, believing fullheartedly he had earned it because no one else had the courage to do what he did.

"So I ask you again, and I advise you to answer carefully," Stefan continued, his voice echoing with power now. "Do you doubt me?"

One of the formerly grumbling advisors answered quickly. "No, sire."

Satisfied, Stefan leaned back against his throne. He drew in a breath and then glanced at Queen Leila, seeing the encouragement in those warm eyes of hers. "I will carry forth King Henry's legacy and he will live on through his daughter, now my wife, and the children we will have."

Suddenly, there was a flurry of activity in the back of the room. Three small chattering pixies flew in, interrupting his speech.

"Beautiful vaulted ceilings!" Thistlewit observed.

"Never mind vaulted—they have ceilings!" Knotgrass replied.

"And real gowns!" Flittle said, looking at Queen Leila's flowing dress. "This is paradise!"

The pixies flew straight toward Stefan, hovering in front of him when they'd reached their goal. He shifted nervously. Creatures from the Moors here in his castle. He wondered if Maleficent had sent these winged fools. And what could they possibly want?

"Who are you?" he asked.

Knotgrass performed a small flourish in the air. "Greetings, Your Majesty," she said. "I am Knotgrass of the Moorland Fair Folk."

Not wanting to be outdone, Flittle flew closer. "I'm Flittle, Your Kingship." Then she nudged Thistlewit.

"And I'm Thistlewit, Your Royalnesses." The smallest of the three bowed as low as she could while she hovered.

"Why have you come?" Stefan demanded.

Knotgrass turned to Flittle. "Tell him, Flittle."

"Why don't you tell him?" Flittle asked.

Stefan grunted impatiently.

"Ugh! You're impossible." Knotgrass threw her hands up. Then, to Stefan, she said, "If Your Grace obliges, we would like to live here. We seek asylum."

Stefan blinked in surprise. He didn't know what he'd been expecting them to ask, but this wasn't it. "Asylum? Why?"

"We don't really love wars," Thistlewit explained.

"And you have ceilings!" Flittle gestured up toward the fixtures under discussion.

"And apparently you play dress-up," Thistlewit added, nodding at Queen Leila, who smiled back.

Knotgrass tried to rein in the conversation. "We have

a strong feeling that darkness descends on the Moors."

Stefan took in this information, knowing full well what had caused this change in the place he had once loved to visit. The choking guilt began to flare up again. Once more, he pushed it down, convincing himself that he'd been in the right to take the actions he had. This was the life he was meant to lead, one that he had worked hard to make for himself. Anyone who stood in his way was nothing more than an obstacle to be overcome.

"And it's very wet and moldy there," Thistlewit added.

"Dank, actually," Flittle said, correcting her. "And smelly. Not here. Here it's fresh as a baby's bottom." She breathed in deeply to make her point.

"The baby's bottom that we wish for you and the queen. We wish that a baby will soon grace your family," Knotgrass said.

In rapid succession the other two pixies added to this new thread of the conversation.

"But not just any old wish. We have magic!"

"And are very good with children!"

Leila smiled broadly and looked at Stefan. His gaze softened. He knew that their presence would make her happy.

With a wave of his hand, he dismissed them. "Fine. You may stay."

The pixies curtsied and flew off, cheering loudly.

"No more bog!" Thistlewit cried.

"I get first choice of lodging!" Knotgrass said.

"What's that smell?" Flittle added, sniffing the air, which, to her, no longer had the appealing scent of a baby's bottom.

Outside, the patient raven cawed and took flight, ready to return to his mistress.

CHAPTER TEN

With Diaval to be her eyes and
ears, Maleficent was no longer in
the dark. A wave of her hand and
he could be changed back into a
raven, allowing him to fly over the countryside with ease and gather news of the
kingdom.

Returning home from his first flight to the castle, Diaval flapped down into the ruins. As soon as
Maleficent turned him back into a human, he began to
tell her the news he'd learned.

"Mistress, Henry's dead. Apparently, he decreed
Stefan would succeed him," Diaval reported to
Maleficent.

A look of pain flashed across her face. As the
information sank in, Maleficent clenched her fist, her

long nails digging into her palm. The truth of Stefan's betrayal was now crystal clear.

"Now he will be king! He did this to me so he would be king!" It infuriated her that his betrayal continued to surprise her. How had she not seen this coming? He was just like every other human, trying to steal to have more. More riches, more land, more power. Letting out a piercing scream, she raised her staff, shooting a lightning bolt into the dark sky.

"Now what, mistress?" Diaval asked.

Her rage purged for the moment, Maleficent slowly lowered her staff, panting and exhausted from the effort. She had been a fool to think the trouble with the humans was over. History was repeating itself once again. It was only a matter of time before Stefan and his army came after the Moors. He knew better than Henry what riches lay there. And that meant it was time to go home.

Maleficent and Diaval arrived at the beautiful Faerie Mound in the center of the Moors as night fell. The plants were brittle and brown, clearly undernourished; the streams had stopped flowing, pooling into dark, dirty spots of water; many of the creatures lay about listlessly. The energy in the atmosphere seemed to have been sucked dry. It was clear that the faerie world had begun to unravel in the weeks during which Maleficent had been gone, and was now in rough shape. But that was all about to change.

Stepping forward, Maleficent made her way toward the Mound. On her shoulder, Diaval the raven squawked nervously as all around her the faeries began to whisper. "Her wings!" one said to another. "They're gone!" a dew faerie whispered loudly.

Maleficent ignored them, gliding to the center of the Mound, a hard look in her eye. Dead tree branches suddenly rose from the ground, writhing together like snakes. They formed a tall throne behind Maleficent, and she lowered herself onto it while keeping her gaze in front of her.

The Fair Folk looked up at her cold gaze, the command in her presence. She was barely recognizable anymore. They bowed to her instinctually, quaking in fear. The Moors had a self-appointed leader now.

Across the grove, Robin observed the scene, hovering in the brush. He wanted to fly to Maleficent's side, to comfort her, to tell her one of their old jokes, to make her face crinkle in a familiar smile. But he knew it would be pointless. Maleficent had grown embittered and dark. Whatever she'd been through had changed her completely. The only thing he and the other Fair Folk could do now was stay out of her way. Tears welled up in his bright eyes as he flew away from the scene. He'd lost Hermia and Lysander long before. And now he felt he'd lost Maleficent.

Over the next year, Maleficent hardly noticed that the other Fair Folk seemed wary of her. She spent most of her time alone or with Diaval, who she sent on nearly daily missions to the castle to bring back any news, hearing all about Stefan's new life as king, and his beautiful wife, King Henry's daughter. It took all Maleficent's energy to quell the infuriating surge of hurt within her. Maleficent had more important things to think about, such as the well-being of the Moors, and just what Stefan would do when he had settled in at the castle. While she was doing all she could to keep the Moors safe and had brought some semblance of peace and restored order, she remained pensive and often distracted. It was hard to focus on the Moors when danger was so close.

She was sitting on her throne, rubbing its rough edges, when Diaval returned from one of his trips. Waving her hand, she transformed him into a human. He stood in front of her, nervously twitching and scratching at his skin. Even though he had been changed dozens of times, he still had a hard time adjusting to the human form. However, that day he seemed even more uncomfortable.

"Tell me," Maleficent said, instantly on the alert.

"I've been to the castle," Diaval began.

Maleficent sighed. "I know," she said, trying to remain patient. "I sent you there. Tell me what you saw."

"I *saw* nothing," he answered, running his hands through his hair. "But I heard . . ." He coughed nervously. "There's been a . . ." His voice trailed off.

"What?" Maleficent demanded. She was growing impatient.

"A . . . um . . ." He looked down at his feet, then up, his eyes meeting the intense stare of Maleficent's. "There's been a . . ." He pretended to see something on his shoulder and flicked at it.

That was it. Maleficent couldn't take any more. *"Speak!"* she commanded.

Diaval snapped to attention. "Child," he said. "King Stefan and the queen have had a child."

"Oh?" Maleficent said, at once surprised by the wave of jealousy that washed over her and angry that Stefan could still affect her feelings that way.

Sensing that Maleficent was unhappy, Diaval plunged ahead, his words running into one another in his rush to get them out—and then get far, far away. "There will be a christening in one month's time. They say it's to be a grand celebration."

se

A celebration? For a baby? It is all just so wonderful, isn't it? she thought. *They will parade Stefan's baby around like a prize. The baby that is the result of so much betrayal and so much pain. Another human put on the Earth to harm and destroy our kind. Oh yes, it is just so wonderful.* Maleficent's lip curled.

But not if she had anything to do with it . . .

CHAPTER ELEVEN

THE DAY OF THE CHRISTENING ARRIVED. THE CASTLE WAS BUSTLING WITH ACTIVITY AS SERVANTS RACED TO AND FRO, DECORATING THE HALLS AND SWEEPING ROOMS LONG SINCE USED. The head housekeeper, normally the picture of control, ran around flinging orders at her staff while the king's personal valet made sure every piece of His Highness's clothing was pristine.

In the massive kitchen, a fire roared under dozens of pots filled with bubbling soups and sauces. The smells wafted through the room, mixing with the aromas of chicken and duck, cookies and cake. Nearly every surface was covered in flour, yet every dish that went out the door was perfectly plated on gleaming white porcelain plates. No expense had been spared. The guests would dine like never before.

Outside, great care had been taken to make sure everything was perfect. The large trees that stood in front of the castle's main door had been sheared into immaculate cones. The horses in their stalls had been groomed until their coats shone, and even the hunting dogs had been given a bath and a brushing. The castle walls had been decked out as well. Long blue banners hung from the dozen towers, and on the soft gray stone connecting each one hung even more of the royal banners. The drawbridge had been lowered and Stefan's flag hung from the archway, waving in the gentle breeze. More festive flags flew from the top of the castle while trumpeters stood on the battlements, heralding the infant. Below, carriages were parked for miles, their passengers dispatched to partake in the huge event.

Inside the Great Hall, hundreds of candles had been lit on the chandeliers that dominated the room, casting a warm glow on the stone floor and walls. A large stained glass window that rose into the arched ceiling forty feet above added muted light for the hundreds of people who had gathered. They were all dressed in their finest, standing shoulder to shoulder, their eyes focused on the podium upon which two huge thrones were perched.

In front of the thrones stood King Stefan and Queen Leila. The queen glowed with pride as she looked down at the infant sleeping in the bassinet. Out of habit, Leila reached up and fingered the bright stone pendant that Stefan had given her when they were first married. She had never seen anything like it, a jewel that seemed to have been made by the sun itself. Catching her playing with the jewelry, Stefan smiled and leaned down to whisper something into her ear.

Well hidden in the back of the crowded room, Maleficent watched Stefan smile at Leila and grimaced. She couldn't hear what they were saying, but she could see them clearly enough. And what she saw on the queen's neck was a stone from the jewel pond—another precious item Stefan had stolen from the Moors. *How dare he!* Maleficent's hands twitched eagerly.

She watched as Knotgrass, Thistlewit, and Flittle approached the baby. They looked older and perhaps a bit plumper, but otherwise they appeared the same.

Stefan isn't the only one to have fooled the kingdom, Maleficent mused. Simple humans. So scared of magic, yet so in love with tricks. They probably thought the pixies adorable, with their little wings and harmless magic. Shaking her head in disgust, Maleficent waited to see what they would do next.

Knotgrass was the first to say something. "Sweet Aurora," she began. "I wish for you the gift of beauty." Reaching down, she touched the sleeping baby's blond curls.

Aurora? So that was the baby human's name, Maleficent thought. Surely Stefan hadn't been the one to name her. It was actually a nice name. It meant "dawn," which was Maleficent's favorite time of day. She shook her head. Now was not the time to be pondering the definition of a name. She turned her attention back to the bassinet.

Next Flittle granted a wish. "My wish," she said, "is that you'll never be blue, only happy all the days of your life."

Finally, Thistlewit stepped forward. "Dear baby," she began. "I wish you . . . I wish you . . ."

Maleficent could no longer idly stand by. Raising her staff, she sent a frigid wind whistling through the hall. Headpieces and clothes were blown about, and the crowd let out scared cries. Thunder cracked and lightning flashed and a dark gray smoke filled the hall. When it cleared, Maleficent stood there, her head held tall, her horns held high. On her shoulder sat Diaval.

The room erupted in whispers as the assembled court tried to figure out who this strange creature was. But one person knew for sure.

"Maleficent!" Stefan cried, his hand at his throat.

She raised an eyebrow. "Well, well. Quite a glittering assemblage, *King* Stefan," she sneered. "Royalty, nobility, the gentry, and, how quaint . . ." She paused and pointed at the three smaller pixies. "Even the rabble." She turned and looked at the queen. "What a pretty necklace. I really feel quite distressed at not receiving an invitation."

"You're not welcome here," Stefan said, puffing out his chest while beside him Leila brushed the stone at her neck with her fingers.

"Not welcome? Oh dear, what an awkward situation." Maleficent turned, as if to leave.

Behind her, Queen Leila spoke up, her royal upbringing getting the best of her. She knew who Maleficent was. She had heard the stories from her father and then from Stefan. They had called Maleficent cruel and evil. But she seemed almost agreeable at the moment. "And you're not offended?"

Maleficent turned back. "Oh, why, no, Your Majesty," she said, her long fingers fluttering at her heart as she moved closer to the bassinet. "And to show you I bear no ill will, I, *too*, shall bestow a gift on the baby."

Stepping in front of Maleficent, Stefan tried to block her. But Maleficent moved past him easily.

"Stay away from the princess!" Knotgrass said, standing protectively in front of the bassinet.

Maleficent laughed. "Gnats," she said. One by one she flicked them out of her way. Then she leaned over and looked into the bassinet. Baby Aurora smiled at her, her cherubic face as adorable as anything Maleficent had ever seen. In that instant, anger and jealousy swirled inside her like a tempest. She would never have a baby that beautiful. She would probably never have a baby at all. No one to care for. No one to carry on her mother's wings or her father's green eyes to a new generation. She *could* have, but that option had been taken away from her when Stefan betrayed her.

Whipping around, Maleficent angrily threw up her arms and addressed the crowd. "Listen well, all of you," she intoned. "The princess shall indeed grow in grace and beauty, beloved by all who know her. . . ."

"That's a lovely gift," the queen said, still oblivious to what was really going on. Oblivious to the true history of Maleficent and Stefan.

Putting a finger to Leila's lips, Maleficent shook her head. She wasn't finished. Not quite yet. There was one final part to her gift. "But before the sun sets on her sixteenth birthday, she will . . ." She paused and looked around the room for inspiration. Her eyes landed on one of the presents brought for the baby. She continued. ". . . prick her finger on the spindle of a spinning wheel and fall into a sleep like death. A sleep from which she will *never* awaken."

As Maleficent's words lingered in the air, the gathered crowd let out a collective gasp. Ignoring them, she turned to go. But Stefan's voice stopped her.

"Maleficent," he said, stepping forward. "Don't do this. I'm begging you."

At the word *begging*, Maleficent raised one eyebrow. Groveling was so unlike Stefan. Slowly, she turned back around to face him. Her expression was cold as she eyed the only person she had ever loved. His eyes pleaded with her and she saw genuine fear and pain in them. But it mattered not at all. Her heart was frozen. There was irony in the situation. The pain she caused him now was so much like the pain he had caused her . . . over and over again. Finally, she responded. "I like begging," she said. "I do. Do it again."

Stefan peered around the room, aware that his subjects watched his every move. Aware that Maleficent was humiliating him. While he wanted to deny her, he had no choice. His infant daughter's future was at stake. "I beg you," he said through clenched teeth.

"All right," Maleficent replied, shrugging as she threw the king a bone. "The princess *can* be woken from her death sleep, but only by"—here she paused and narrowed her gaze so that the next words she spoke pierced Stefan to the core—"True Love's Kiss."

She almost laughed when she said the words. She had learned from Stefan that things like true love did not exist. "This curse will last until the end of time. No power on Earth can change it." She turned and began to leave. Behind her, Stefan signaled his guards to attack. But the wind Maleficent had conjured picked up, keeping the guards and guests at bay. In front of her, the door to the throne room blew open. A moment later, Maleficent disappeared through it, leaving panic and chaos in her wake.

As she made her way back to the Moors, she smiled.

When she had entered the castle, she had been unsure of what she would do when the time came. She hadn't known about the gifts the pixies would bestow. Or even how she would feel when once more so close to Stefan. A small part of her had been worried she would be too frightened to do anything at all. But what happened in the end, Maleficent thought, couldn't have turned out better. It was priceless. An unbreakable curse that was sure to drive Stefan mad and throw the kingdom into mayhem. It was perfect. Absolutely perfect.

Evening had fallen and the night sky was full of stars when Maleficent returned to the Moors. She was energized by the day's events, and an idea began to form in her head, one to keep the human aggressors out of their land for good. She turned and walked to the very edge of the Moors, where faerie land met human land. Taking a deep breath, she closed her eyes and concentrated on the magic that flowed within her. It had been growing stronger for a while. As she walked through the Moors now, her body called out to the land around her, pulling from its energy, making her stronger. She found that she could even focus on certain flora and fauna and extract magic directly from the individual plants and animals. *Which,* she thought with a smile, *is very useful.*

Slowly, she began to speak to the ground. She called out to the grasses and to the roots that lay beneath the soil. She spoke to the trees nearby, asking them to lend their magic, to help her protect the Moors. Magic pulsed all around her, and the air shimmered. As she lifted her arms, dark twisted branches covered with sharp thorns began to rise out of the earth. They sped toward the sky and intertwined with each other, braiding their thick trunks together. As they did so, a wall began to form. The wall continued to grow until it was impossible to see from one side to the other. It grew until its thorns stuck out in all directions, their sharp tips gleaming black. It grew until it rose nearly forty feet in the air. It grew until it was impenetrable.

When Maleficent opened her eyes, the magic stopped flowing from her. She stepped back and nodded. The wall wasn't pretty, but it would have to do.

Satisfied with her work, Maleficent went back to her throne on the Mound. She glanced at the landscape around her, reveling in the beauty and tranquility of the Moors, which had been restored in her time as ruler there. The other Fair Folk even seemed more comfortable around her, going on with their daily activities without shuddering or flying away whenever she was close by. However, her old friends, Robin included, continued to stay away. Maleficent strangely understood this. She'd lost her friendships as soon as she'd lost her wings and her old sense of self. She was a new faerie now.

In the peaceful silence of the Faerie Mound, she found her mind wandering outside of life at the Moors. She now had time to reflect upon the day's events. It had felt oh so nice to see Stefan suffer. And casting this curse would help the Moors, too. A weakened human kingdom meant less threat to them, and there was no way Stefan hadn't been weakened by the curse placed on his only daughter.

Feeling a judgmental gaze, Maleficent looked to her side. Diaval, in his human form, stood there, staring at her. She ignored him and went back to relishing her revenge. But Diaval continued to glare at her, silently chastising her for what she had done. A part of her wanted to try to explain to him that she wasn't being mean to the baby. She wanted to tell Diaval how badly Stefan had hurt her and how much it still ached, every day, and that that was why she had done what she did. But she couldn't admit that to him. And she certainly couldn't wait for him to start expressing his disapproval. So instead, she simply waved a hand and transformed him into a raven. He could caw all he wanted but he wouldn't be able to reprimand her.

CHAPTER TWELVE

WHILE IT WOULD HAVE BEEN NICE TO KEEP DIAVAL AS A RAVEN FOR A LONG PERIOD OF TIME, MALEFICENT KNEW SHE NEEDED HIM TO INFORM HER OF GOINGS-ON IN THE KINGDOM. In the wake of her christening present to Aurora, Maleficent was eager to hear what Stefan would do to protect his infant daughter. So she continued to send Diaval on his reconnaissance missions and transform him when he returned.

She didn't have to wait long for news.

A few days after Aurora's celebration, Diaval flew back to the Faerie Mound. He landed in front of Maleficent's throne and hopped around, flapping his wings furiously until she transformed him. When he was human once more, he quickly filled in his mistress on what he had witnessed.

Stefan, it seemed, was not taking Maleficent's "gift" lightly. He'd ordered his men to gather all the spinning wheels in the kingdom and lock them in the dungeons. While the queen was not pleased, the king also had ordered the three pixies to whisk Aurora away from the kingdom. His hope was to keep her hidden and safe, protected by faerie magic and a lack of spinning wheels. Stefan thought no one but his closest advisors knew his plan. But of course, he was wrong. For Diaval had seen Knotgrass, Thistlewit, and Flittle on their way out of the kingdom. He had seen them use their magic to make themselves grow to the size of regular humans, and he had followed them while they made their way to a small cottage in the middle of the woods that surrounded the castle. Then, he told Maleficent, he had flown back to the Faerie Mound as fast as he could.

When Diaval finally stopped talking, Maleficent shook her head. "Idiots," she said. Diaval nodded in agreement and then paused. He wasn't sure who she meant—the king and queen or the pixies themselves.

"Those three raising a baby? What a disaster! I must see this for myself."

Maleficent stood, grabbing her staff, and began walking. Diaval hurried to catch up. But he was used to flying, so his gait was slower and he kept tripping. Raising a hand, Maleficent turned Diaval back into a raven so he could keep up, and quickly made her way to the Thorn Wall at the edge of the Moors.

Maleficent was capable of parting the thorny branches to allow herself passage between the human and faerie worlds. While she didn't like to leave the Moors, she had found herself beyond their borders too often of late. *I don't want to make a habit of this,* she thought as she walked through the Wall and let it close behind her. *I'll just take a quick look at the baby and that will be all. Then I will be done. I'll let the curse play out and that will be that.*

Following Diaval, who flew above and slightly ahead of Maleficent, she made her way deeper and deeper into the human forest. Tall trees rose into the air and thick green vegetation covered the ground. Unlike the Faerie

Moors, which were inhabited by more types of creatures than ever, the human land seemed oddly empty. After a while, the pair arrived at a clearing. In the middle stood a small cottage with a thatched roof and white sides crisscrossed with brown beams. It was clear that the cottage had been abandoned for quite some time. Upon closer inspection Maleficent could make out holes in the thatch, and weeds grew tall among what once had been an herb garden. Hidden in the shadows of the trees that surrounded the clearing, Maleficent watched as the pixies, now big and awkward in their new bodies, stumbled about, trying to spruce up the place and quickly make it homey and inviting. When they stepped inside to take a break, Maleficent carefully made her way to the side of the cottage. Looking to Diaval, she saw him nod his feathered head at one of the small windows.

Maleficent peered through it and saw baby Aurora tucked in her bassinet, sleeping peacefully. Her lip curled back as she gazed at the baby's soft, rosy cheeks. She looked a bit bigger than when she'd last seen her, a bit plumper, maybe, but just as beautiful. "I could almost feel sorry for it." Beside her, Diaval nodded his raven head.

Suddenly, Aurora opened her eyes and looked directly at Maleficent. In response, Maleficent made a mean face at the baby. Aurora smiled. Maleficent made an even meaner face. Aurora laughed and began to clap her hands.

"I hate you," Maleficent said.

She was about to try to make the scariest face she could when she heard the loud bustle of the three pixies approaching. Quickly, she backed away from the window.

The three pixies entered Aurora's room and made their way to the bassinet. Immediately, the baby began to cry. Maleficent listened as the pixies argued among themselves about what they should do before finally deciding Aurora was hungry. They then proceeded to plop a whole banana, apple, and orange in with the baby before walking out of the room. Aurora's screams grew louder.

"It's going to starve with those three looking after it," Maleficent muttered. *But that's not my problem,* she added silently. She turned and walked away, her shoulders tense until the sound of Aurora's cries finally faded.

For the next few weeks, Aurora was the least of Maleficent's concerns, though she knew Diaval visited the baby every day. What he did while he was there, she didn't know. But it felt a bit like a betrayal, in any event.

Nevertheless, Maleficent's focus was on King Stefan and his castle. On a daily basis she heard reports from Diaval that Stefan was said to be going mad in the wake of her curse. He was paranoid. Convinced that Maleficent would come back any day to wreak further damage and destruction, he had all his soldiers at the ready. He sent them to the Thorn Wall over and over again, hoping they could chop it down. Once, the soldiers had even catapulted large fireballs, trying to burn it down. But the Wall remained impenetrable, just as Maleficent had planned, and the thorny vines stopped the greedy humans in their tracks. Her parents had thought talk and reasoning could keep the humans from invading. But now it was more than evident that this—this barrier, this violence—was the only way.

One morning, as Maleficent sat on her throne, contemplating how much things had changed since that long-ago day when she had met Stefan at the jewel pool, Diaval landed on the Mound. Transforming him back into a man, Maleficent waited for his daily report.

"You saw nothing?" she asked when he finished his report.

Diaval shook his head. "No, mistress," he said softly, aware that this would not make Maleficent happy. "The castle is locked up tight. I couldn't see inside." He went on to explain that in fear of another visit from Maleficent, Stefan had ordered windows to be boarded up, the drawbridge to be raised, and all entrances to be guarded by double the men. He was not taking any chances.

Maleficent's fist clenched tightly around the top of her staff. She despised Stefan. Pure and simple. "He's hiding from me," she said, sneering. "He always was a coward. Fine. Let him rot in there. His child is doomed and there's nothing he can do about it."

Standing beside her, Diaval kept quiet, waiting for Maleficent to do what she always inevitably did—turn him into a raven so he wouldn't ask questions or bother her. Maleficent felt his gaze on her but ignored it. Lately, she hadn't wanted to transform him. She knew that he would go and visit Aurora as soon as he had wings. And for some reason, that irked Maleficent.

Growing impatient, Diaval tapped Maleficent on the shoulder to get her attention. Turning, she looked down at the spot where his fingers had brushed her shoulder, an unreadable expression on her face. "What is it?" she asked.

"Aren't you going to change me?" he retorted.

"Why?" Maleficent queried, curious if he would tell her the real reason.

But instead of saying he wanted to see Aurora, he replied, "I prefer my own form."

Shrugging, Maleficent waved her hand and transformed Diaval back into a raven. With a caw, he rose into the air and began to fly away. But Maleficent's voice stopped him. "Diaval," she called. Veering, he flew back. When he was once more in front of her, she added, "Are you going to stay close or do I have to put you in a cage?"

His feathers ruffled, Diaval flew over and landed on top of Maleficent's staff. It seemed his trip to the cottage would have to wait.

CHAPTER THIRTEEN

WHILE MALEFICENT HATED TO ADMIT IT, DIAVAL WASN'T THE ONLY ONE WHO WAS CURIOUS ABOUT THE BABY. AS THE DAYS TURNED INTO WEEKS AND THEN INTO MONTHS, THE CURIOSITY ATE AT MALEFICENT. It ate at her while she wandered the Moors, checking on the Thorn Wall. It ate at her while she sat on her throne, listening to the buzzing of faeries complaining or gossiping. The curiosity nearly overwhelmed her when she stumbled upon a bird and her newly hatched babies, their little beaks jabbing at the air helplessly. And when she saw three pixies that bore an uncanny resemblance to Knotgrass, Thistlewit, and Flittle in the middle of a fight that caused them to ignore their little faerie children, the curiosity got the best of her.

Before she could think twice, she found herself parting the Wall and making her way into the forest.

With purposeful strides, she moved toward the cottage in the clearing. Arriving, Maleficent saw that the back door was wide open and the pixies were nowhere in sight. But Aurora was. The infant had grown into a beautiful toddler with soft blond curls and rosy cheeks. As Maleficent watched, Aurora backed herself down the two steps and then began to toddle about. She burbled and giggled to herself, clearly used to being alone. *Something we have in common,* Maleficent thought, despite herself.

Determined to get over her curiosity, Maleficent approached the baby. Leaning down, she made the scariest face she could and screamed, *"Ahhhhh!"*

It worked! The baby began to wail and throw her arms about. Smiling, Maleficent waited for Aurora to run away. And sure enough, the baby did run. But to her surprise, Aurora ran straight at her. Then she threw her little arms around Maleficent's legs and buried her head in the faerie's long dark robes.

"Off! Off!" Maleficent cried, pushing Aurora away as

though she were a bug. But the baby just threw herself right back on Maleficent and continued to cry piteously. Then Aurora raised her arms, silently begging to be picked up.

Maleficent glanced around. Despite the loud wails, no one seemed to be coming. And if no one was coming, that meant the baby was going to keep crying. And all that crying was giving her a terrible headache. . . .

But no, Maleficent resolved. She would not fall for the big blue watery eyes that looked up at her hopefully. She folded her arms across her chest and shook her head. Aurora kept crying. Before she could stop herself, Maleficent leaned down and picked up the wailing child. "Shut your mouth," she said, though her tone was softer than the words she uttered.

Instantly, Aurora melted into Maleficent. Wrapping her pudgy arms around Maleficent's neck, she whimpered and gasped for a moment. As Aurora calmed down, Maleficent tried to ignore the warm feeling spreading through her body. She tried to ignore the fresh scent of Aurora's hair. She tried not to feel the fluttering heartbeat against her own chest and the way it made her instinctively want to tighten her grip and keep the baby safe. This was the enemy. She had to stay strong.

Then Aurora let out an adorable babble and, with absolutely no fear, reached up and grabbed one of Maleficent's horns. Shocked, Maleficent pulled her head back. Aurora's bottom lip quivered a bit. Curious to see what she would do next, Maleficent slowly bent her head ever so slightly. Aurora's lip stopped quivering instantly and once more she let out a giggle and latched on, completely unafraid.

It was too much for Maleficent. Quickly she put Aurora down and, without looking back, left the clearing. But as she made her way back to the Faerie Mound, her mind was racing. She couldn't deny it. Aurora was sort of, kind of, maybe just a *little* cute. And that she even thought that at all made Maleficent furious at herself. Because she couldn't afford to think the baby was cute or sweet or cuddly or precious. No. She had cursed her to eternal sleep. So there was no point in even paying attention to Aurora. Was there?

Yet as the saying goes, the best-laid plans often go wrong, and Maleficent quickly found that she couldn't help keeping an eye on Aurora. Diaval didn't help the situation, either. Growing bolder about his attachment to the infant, he now dragged Maleficent along with him when he went to watch Aurora—which he had to do, often. The three pixies were useless, more concerned with themselves than with the baby they had been charged to protect. Oftentimes, as she and Diaval watched from the shadows, Maleficent would overhear them bemoaning their lot in life, stuck in the awkward human-sized bodies, out in the middle of nowhere, unable to partake in the royal trappings, and forbidden by Stefan to use magic unless absolutely necessary. They occasionally paid attention to Aurora, but for the most part, the baby fended for herself.

One particularly beautiful afternoon, Maleficent

reclined in a tree next to Diaval, who kept a raven eye on Aurora as she played below. Nearby, the pixies had laid out a picnic. Fresh berries, bread, and cheese lay neatly on a brightly colored towel. But Aurora wanted nothing to do with the food. She was having too much fun playing with the butterflies that were flittering around nearby.

Glancing over and watching the baby play, Maleficent was struck, not for the first time, by Aurora's complete innocence. The baby had no idea what her future held. She had no clue what her father had done or who her mother had married. Aurora just knew that that day it was sunny and there were butterflies to chase. Maleficent felt anger bubble up in her chest. She had been that innocent once, that trusting and carefree. And look what it had gotten her. Shaking her head to clear her negative thoughts, Maleficent tossed a nut to Diaval. She needed to amuse herself with something other than thoughts about her past. Something to remind her that she was free to do what she wanted, when she wanted.

Noticing that the pixies had all sat down and were lounging lazily in the warm sun, Maleficent smiled mischievously. She made a tiny gesture, mimicking the movement of pulling someone's hair. On the ground below, Thistlewit let out a yelp.

The faerie immediately looked next to her, convinced that Flittle had pulled her hair. In retaliation, she pulled a strand of Flittle's hair—hard. Soon the three pixies were in the midst of an all-out hair-tugging war. With a satisfied smile, Maleficent leaned back and tossed a nut into her mouth.

For a moment, Maleficent just sat there, reveling in the shrieks and cries from the three pixies below. Robin would have been proud of her trickery—maybe there *was* some of the old Maleficent left somehow. Suddenly, out of the corner of her eye, she noticed Aurora chasing a butterfly. The baby's little feet pounded on the warm grass, her hands were out in front of her, and her fingers grabbed frantically. Looking ahead, Maleficent raised an eyebrow. Intent on catching the butterfly, Aurora was oblivious that she was heading straight toward danger.

"The little beast is about to fall off that ledge," Maleficent said nonchalantly to Diaval.

With a worried *"awk,"* Diaval flew off the branch and to the pixies for help. He began to caw wildly, flying around their blanket. Unfortunately, Knotgrass, Thistlewit, and Flittle were far too absorbed in their fight even to give notice to Diaval, shooing him away absentmindedly as they continued to bicker.

Meanwhile, Maleficent watched as Aurora continued to run headlong toward the ledge. She was only fifty feet away. Then forty. Then thirty. Maleficent glanced over her shoulder and saw that the pixies still had no clue what was going on and Diaval was still cawing madly. The coast was clear. Quickly, she made her way out of the tree and raced over to the baby. Just as Aurora's little foot took a step into nothing, Maleficent grabbed the baby and pulled her back. Seeing Maleficent's familiar face, Aurora smiled.

Maleficent quickly plopped Aurora down safely and then retreated to the tree. A moment later Diaval landed next to her. Giving up on the pixies, he had flown over to try to help Aurora but found her safe and sound. Now he glanced at Maleficent and cocked his head, a quizzical look in his eyes.

"What?" she asked innocently. So she had saved Aurora's life. What was the big deal? It certainly didn't mean she liked the brat or anything.

CHAPTER FOURTEEN

Time passed quickly in the forest, and before long, Aurora was no longer a toddler but a child of eight. The dangerous baby years were over, and while the pixies had been practically useless to an infant, they seemed capable enough of taking care of a young girl. So Maleficent mostly stayed in the Moors, safe from humans and content in the knowledge that Stefan, as all of Diaval's reports indicated, was a sad, mad, lonely king. But on occasion, she would make a visit to see Aurora.

Once, when Aurora was still a toddler, Maleficent had followed Diaval to the clearing and waited in the shadows of the trees as, in raven form, Diaval played with the girl. Fall had turned the leaves gold and red and sent many of them drifting to the ground. Aurora, her blond hair long and loose, sat in the midst of a big pile of leaves, giggling. She lifted a handful and threw them into the air, laughing as a few landed on the black bird. Reaching out, she gently stroked Diaval's thick black feathers. "What a pretty bird," she said, her voice pleasant to the ear.

Maleficent squirmed. At one time, the baby had been the only thing to irk her. Yet more and more, she found that Diaval's spending time with Aurora irked her far more. Or was she irked because he could play with her out in the open, with such ease? That afternoon Maleficent had shaken her head to clear the ridiculous thought and walked away from the clearing.

Yet she was never gone for very long. Even though she hated to admit it, she felt an odd pull to Aurora. And there was another draw, as well. It was too much temptation to play tricks on the three pixies, a break from her serious thoughts and a brief reminder of happier days spent playing tricks on the other faeries with Robin. Often the thought of disrupting the little pixies' lives for even a few moments was enough to send Maleficent through the Wall and into the human forest.

One summer morning she and Diaval, in his human form, made their way to the clearing. Hearing Knotgrass's nasally voice, Maleficent inched up to the edge of the cottage. Diaval followed and together they peered through an open window. On the other side, the three pixies were sitting at the kitchen table playing a game of checkers. As usual, they were bickering.

"What's this?" Flittle said, reaching out and grabbing Knotgrass's hand. Prying it open, she revealed one of the markers. "You're cheating!"

"I resent the insinuation," Knotgrass huffed.

"There's no insinuation. I've caught you in the act," Flittle retorted. "You cheating hedgepig."

As the three began to hurl insults at one another, Maleficent raised a finger. A single drop of water fell onto Knotgrass's head. She brushed it away absently.

Plink! Another drop fell. Again, Knotgrass brushed away the water.

Plink! Plink! Plink! Unable to ignore the water any longer, Knotgrass looked up, trying to see where it was coming from. Not seeing an obvious leak, she moved over. But it was no use. *Plink! Plink!* More drops fell, landing only on Knotgrass.

Shooting a dirty look at Flittle, Knotgrass snapped, "Stop doing that!"

"I'm not doing anything," Flittle protested.

Hiding on the other side of the window, Maleficent stifled a laugh. It was so easy to rattle the pixies. Her shoulders shook as they tried to figure out the origin of the water, blaming each other and then a leak. But as Knotgrass pointed out, a leak would only happen if it was raining. And it most definitely wasn't raining.

Plink! Plink! Plink! Plink!

The drops came faster and faster, each one falling only on Knotgrass. Finally, she slammed her hand down on the table. "Stop it!" she screamed.

Instantly, the drops ceased. Knotgrass anxiously stared at the ceiling as though waiting for the next wave. But when, after a few moments, no more water fell, she sighed and sat down.

And then it poured.

A torrent of water fell on Knotgrass, drenching her

instantly. The other two pixies began to laugh, but as they did, a wave of water poured down the stairs, washing over them. They all screamed.

Outside, Maleficent was racked with laughter. Her body shook and she struggled not to make a sound as she waved her hand again. Inside the cottage thunder boomed and lightning cracked. Looking at Diaval next to her, Maleficent smiled, eager for him to join in the fun, to be her partner in crime as Robin had been so many years earlier. But his expression was serious.

"Oh, come on," Maleficent said. "That is funny!"

Diaval didn't respond right away and Maleficent could tell he was working up the courage to speak. Finally, he cleared his throat. "Mistress," he began, "there's something I need to know."

Maleficent let out a sigh. He was ruining all her fun. "And what is that?" she asked, not bothering to hide her aggravation. What possibly could be so important that Diaval would take away from one of the few carefree moments Maleficent allowed herself?

His next question shocked the smirk right off her

face. "When are you planning to revoke your curse?"

"Who said I was planning on revoking it?" she asked, turning her attention back to the cottage. "I hate that little beast."

Diaval shook his head. He had expected Maleficent to be difficult. "You hate *Stefan*," he pointed out. "May I speak freely?"

"No," Maleficent answered. Waving her hand, she moved to transform him. But for once, Diaval didn't let her. He grabbed her hand, his fingers lacing with hers.

"Any time you don't like what I have to say, you change me back into a bird," he pointed out.

Maleficent opened her mouth to retort but then shook her head, thinking better of it. This was not a conversation to be had there or then. Before he could stop her, Maleficent pulled her hand away. Quickly she waved it, transforming him once more into a raven. When he was muted, she sighed. Diaval had taken all the fun out of the day. And for what? To try to save his little friend? Why had he even bothered? Did he think Maleficent would retract the curse and Aurora could live with them? It was a laughable thought. It was not like Aurora could ever be a part of the Moors. She didn't fit in there. She could *never* fit in there. How could a human understand and appreciate the magic and nature of the Moors? No, it was silly of Diaval. What was done was done. There was no revoking the curse. Maleficent was perfectly content with that. And what she wanted to do then, more than anything, was continue to play with the pixies.

CHAPTER FIFTEEN

MORE YEARS PASSED. SEASONS CAME AND WENT. DAYS GREW LONGER AND THEN SHORTER AND THEN LONGER AGAIN. THE THICK WALL GREW TALLER IN THE SUMMER, INVIGORATED BY THE SUN'S WARMTH. And in fall, the roots dug deeper. On one side, in the Faerie Moors, Maleficent continued to sit on the throne. She focused on helping the Moors thrive and enjoyed knowing that she had brought a long-lasting peace for all the creatures, great and small.

Over the years, Maleficent grew more confident and more beautiful. On the other side of the Thorn Wall, however, things did not go as well. In his castle, King Stefan grew weaker and more paranoid. His beard grew gray and thinned while his belly became larger. His red-rimmed eyes were constantly trained on the wall as he waited for the moment it would show him its weakness. He had ordered the once lovely light stone walls of the castle to be covered by thick, dull iron—an attempt to make sure that Maleficent could be kept out. It gave the castle a scary, foreboding appearance, and those who lived in its shadow felt its heavy weight on their shoulders. Gone were the days of celebrations and fun. The kingdom, many said, was in a perpetual state of mourning for a cursed princess who they would never see grow up.

Deep in the woods between the two worlds, unaware of it all, Aurora grew older. Her pudgy cheeks thinned out yet stayed rosy. The little legs that had so often gotten her into trouble became long and lean so that she towered over her short "aunts." The button nose that turned up slightly at the tip fit her face perfectly, and the long blond locks that flowed down to her tiny waist shimmered and shone. At fifteen, she was a vision of beauty. And raised away from the trappings of royal life, she was a vision of kindness, as well. There was not an animal she didn't love or a bird she didn't sing to. She would wander the woods for hours at a time, lost in thought but perfectly comfortable with the nature around her.

Maleficent had watched as Aurora grew and got closer and closer to the age of her curse. She had witnessed the awkward years when Aurora's legs were too long for her body, and seen the emotional shift from child to teen as Aurora struggled to figure out who she was, never getting answers from the three women who had raised her. She had followed the girl as she wandered the woods, always surprised to see a human so in touch with nature. And she had been uncomfortable when, wandering far from home one afternoon, Aurora had discovered the Wall. Soon Aurora began to spend long afternoons lying in front of it, trying to see through its thick, thorny branches. While Maleficent tried to ignore the girl's presence so close to her home, it was practically impossible. The girl always seemed to be nearby.

Sitting with Diaval one afternoon on the human side of the Wall, Maleficent tried to relax and enjoy lying on the warm ground. Her gaze fell on the road that ran across from the Wall. It was the road between the human forest and the Faerie Moors. Long and winding, it had deep ruts dug into the dirt by countless carriages and wagons. Tall trees grew on either side of it. In the opposite direction was King Stefan's castle. As the road drew closer to the castle, it became more structured, the trees trimmed back and the foliage kept to a minimum. Gazing at Stefan's castle in the distance, Maleficent crinkled her nose. All those years later and the place still made her mad.

Suddenly, Diaval, who was in his human form, cocked his head, listening. "She's back again," he said after a moment.

Pushing themselves back into the shadows of the thick branches, the pair watched as a moment later Aurora emerged from the woods. Looking around to be sure no one had spotted her, Aurora crossed the road and made her way up to the thorns. She craned her neck up, marveling again at the immensity of the Wall. She stood on tiptoe and then sank, trying to find a hole in the Wall to see through.

"Curious little beast," Maleficent muttered as she

watched Aurora. She was just about to signal Diaval to go when there was the loud sound of metal cutting through wood. The noise sliced through Maleficent, causing her to shudder, as though she were the one being cut.

Forgetting all about Aurora, Maleficent began to walk toward the noise. It didn't take her long to discover the source. A large wagon had broken down on the road. Two of its wheels lay flat on the ground, the other two still connected to the disabled vehicle. The back of the wagon was shattered where its heavy cargo had fallen through. Squinting, Maleficent could just make out a hint of heavy iron peering from underneath the cargo cover.

Several soldiers, armed in iron and carrying iron weapons, stood guard near the cargo. Two more had made their way to the edge of the forest and were using a two-handed saw to cut down a tree. They were clearly going to use the fresh wood to repair their wagon.

As the metal blade sliced into the tree's trunk, Maleficent cringed. Anger filled her and she raised her staff, ready to put a stop to the humans' destructive work. But a warning caw from Diaval made her pause. Turning, she saw that Aurora was approaching.

Two of the soldiers had left the group, spotting Aurora close by. The first one called out to her. "Hey, you. What are you doing?"

"You don't belong out here," the other said.

Then they started shouting over each other.

"How did you get out here?"

"Why are you out here in the middle of the forest?"

Aurora started walking in their direction, her eyes curious and trusting.

Maleficent quickly formed a plan in her mind. The soldiers outnumbered her. And they did have iron weapons. But she had magic. And Diaval. Looking at him, she narrowed her eyes. She was going to need something a bit scarier than a raven to help her frighten off the soldiers. Raising her staff, she softly said, "Bring them to me."

With a small cry, Diaval fell to his knees. And then, in front of Maleficent's eyes, he transformed into an enormous wolf. His fur was thick and black and long;

sharp talons extended from huge paws. He was a terrifying creature. The only things that were not frightening were the wolf's eyes, which still retained Diaval's kindness. He bounded off.

The soldiers stopped in their tracks as soon as they heard a loud, echoing howl. Instantly, they turned around and headed back to the other men.

At the same time, Maleficent approached Aurora from behind. She pulled a yellow flower from her robe and blew on it. Pollen flew off the flower, got caught in the gentle breeze, and began to move toward Aurora.

"Sleep," Maleficent said softly.

Taking the shape of a small cloud, the pollen continued to float toward Aurora. Reaching her, the yellow dust swirled around, and her eyes began to close. A moment later, Aurora's body went limp and she gently dropped to the ground. But Aurora was still too visible for Maleficent's liking. Lifting her staff, Maleficent raised the princess's sleeping body slowly into the air. The girl floated higher and higher until she hovered safely above the soldiers' line of sight.

That taken care of, Maleficent turned her attention back to the soldiers. She watched as Diaval galloped closer and closer to them. Terrified of the mass of fur and muscle fast approaching, the soldiers drew their swords. And then, just as swiftly, they started running in the opposite direction. Diaval trailed behind like a menacing sheepdog.

Too late, the soldiers realized they were racing straight toward a tall, horned creature. They skidded to a stop just as Maleficent raised her staff once more, lifting the soldiers into the air this time. Weapons began to rain down on her as she made them float in the air. She twisted her staff, and the soldiers bumped into one another in the air, then fell to the ground in an unconscious heap.

She grinned, satisfied that the crisis had been averted. But the smile faded on her lips as she looked down at an iron helmet lying near her feet. She studied it and then carefully reached out a finger. The tip touched the iron and Maleficent felt a searing heat. She snatched her hand away and held it to her chest. *So that little problem hasn't gone away,* she thought. And if she faced more soldiers in another battle, it could become a much bigger problem.

Her thoughts were interrupted by the return of Diaval. Waving her hand, she transformed him back into a human. His cheeks were flushed and he shuffled from foot to foot, clearly agitated.

"How could you do that to me?" he asked angrily.

Maleficent took a step back, surprised by his response. He had never reacted to a transformation like that before. "You said . . . anything I need," she replied haltingly. And he had. True, it had been many years earlier, but she didn't think there was an expiration date.

"Not a dog!" Diaval snapped.

Maleficent shrugged. So *that* was what he was so upset about. That he had been furry. "It was a wolf," she pointed out, "not a dog."

"It's the same thing," Diaval replied. "They're dirty, vicious, and they hunt birds."

"Fine," Maleficent said, throwing up her hands. "Next time I'll change you into a mealy worm."

She turned and began to make her way back to the Wall. It wouldn't be long before the soldiers awoke and alerted King Stefan to the skirmish. She would be safer in the Moors. Diaval followed, still muttering about his earlier transformation. "I'll be a mealy worm," he was saying. "Gladly! Anything but a filthy, stinking . . . *Awk!*"

Looking over her shoulder, Maleficent tried not to smile as Diaval flapped angrily about. He could be so dramatic. A little transformation never hurt anybody, and it wasn't like he had hurt a bird while he was a wolf.

Suddenly, Maleficent remembered Aurora. Looking up, she saw the princess was still floating in the air, blissfully asleep and unaware of the battle that had occurred on the ground below. She needed to wake the girl up and get her safely back to the cottage before any of Stefan's men woke up. Yet that could take a while and she could be followed if the soldiers were good trackers. Maleficent doubted she had that long. Suddenly, she had an idea. A strange and unsettling idea, but an idea nonetheless.

"I wonder . . ." she mused aloud.

What if she were to take Aurora to the other side of the Wall? The men couldn't follow them there and Aurora would be safe for the time being. *Plus,* Maleficent thought, *I am curious to see what the girl would think of the Moors. Would she see their beauty? Or be frightened? Or overcome with the urge to take and destroy like every other human?* She shook her head. Was she being foolish even to consider taking her to the Moors? Or was it the best decision given the circumstances?

Maleficent could stand there all day battling with herself. But time was precious and she needed to make a decision . . . soon. Lifting her staff, she pointed it at Aurora.

CHAPTER SIXTEEN

Night had fallen on the Moors. High in the sky a full moon hung and beams of light shone down, illuminating the lush ground. The air was still and silent. Most of the Moorland creatures were asleep, some tucked in the leaves on the ground, others resting in trees. Through it all, a sleeping Aurora floated. Maleficent walked a few paces behind while Diaval flew ahead. As the trio made their way along, a few curious faeries peeped out, eager to see who would dare disturb the peaceful wood at that hour.

Arriving at a small glen through which a shallow stream burbled, Maleficent lowered Aurora gently to the ground. Then she slipped into the shadows. She took a deep breath, then whispered, "Awaken."

Maleficent waited, her heart pounding. She was beginning to regret her decision to bring the girl there. What had possessed her? It had seemed like a good idea at the time, but now, as Aurora's eyes fluttered open, Maleficent was beginning to think differently.

Slowly, Aurora sat up. She took in her surroundings calmly with her big blue eyes, as though waking up in an unfamiliar grove of trees was a common event for her. Watching Aurora take in the Moors, Maleficent felt an ache in her chest. She had never felt comfortable out of her familiar surroundings. Yet Aurora, who had lived her whole life in one cottage and knew only three people, seemed unfazed.

Turning her head in Maleficent's direction, Aurora spoke. "I know you're there."

Startled, Maleficent slipped farther back into the shadows.

"Don't be afraid," Aurora added.

"I'm not afraid," Maleficent said defensively. She slapped a hand over her mouth. As soon as the words had slipped out, she wished could take them back. Now there was no hiding.

"Then come out," Aurora pleaded.

Maleficent smiled. Ah, maybe there was a way out of this after all. "Then *you'll* be afraid," she said.

But Aurora shook her head. "No, I won't," she said stubbornly.

It appeared Maleficent had no choice. She hadn't really thought through what would happen once Aurora was in the Moors, but she most *certainly* hadn't thought she would have to talk to the princess. Nevertheless, if Aurora was like any other human, the girl would run away as soon as she saw Maleficent.

Stepping out of the shadows, Maleficent made her way closer. A bright beam of moonlight shot down, illuminating her, and she cast a long shadow on the ground behind her. In the night, her horns looked bigger and darker, and she was not surprised to see Aurora's eyes widen with fear. But what did surprise her was that Aurora didn't run. Instead, she spoke.

"I know who you are," she said, causing Maleficent to raise an eyebrow. "You're my faerie godmother."

A chuckle caught in Maleficent's throat. "Your . . . what?" she asked, trying not to laugh out loud.

Ignoring Maleficent's reaction, Aurora nodded. "Faerie godmother," she repeated slowly. "You've been watching over me my whole life. I've always known you were close by."

"How?" Maleficent asked, curiosity getting the best of her.

Aurora pointed over Maleficent's shoulder. Turning, Maleficent saw her distinct horned shadow. "It's been following me ever since I was small," Aurora explained. "Wherever I went, your shadow was always with me."

Hearing that, Diaval let out a loud caw. While Maleficent knew he was, in his own bird way, saying something along the lines of "I knew it!" Aurora simply heard the birdcall and smiled. Watching as Diaval landed on Maleficent's shoulder, she paused and then made her way closer.

"I remember you!" she said, reaching up to pet Diaval. "Pretty bird."

Maleficent tried not to cringe as the girl's small hand brushed her shoulder. She hadn't been this close to a stranger in a long, long time. To her surprise, it didn't feel as terrible as she would have thought.

And what was even more surprising was how at home Aurora seemed in the glen. She turned from Diaval and wandered around, bending down every now and then to get a closer look at the small flowers and plants that were different from the ones on her side of the Wall.

As she explored, Moorland faeries, awoken from their slumber, began to emerge, curious to see the human in their midst. When Aurora caught sight of the winged creatures, her face filled with wonder. Maleficent felt herself smiling as several courageous dew faeries fluttered up to the princess, their translucent wings glimmering in the moonlight. It had been a long time since Maleficent had really looked at her home. True, she fought to defend it and loved it fiercely, but with Aurora there, she was seeing it in a fresh light. It was beautiful and mysterious. Peaceful and yet alive. The trees protected the plants, and the plants hugged the ground. There was a home and place for everyone and everything. That, Maleficent thought, was why she fought so hard to keep it safe.

Unaware of Maleficent's musings, Aurora softly ran her hand over the top of a cattail. "I've always wanted to come here," she said softly. "But my aunts told me it was forbidden." She looked up, and her eyes met Maleficent's. "How did we get through the Wall?"

The question snapped Maleficent back to reality. It was one thing to have the girl there for a short while, but it would not do to have her asking questions and wanting to come back. "It's time to take you home," Maleficent said, not answering Aurora.

"So soon?" the princess said, clearly disappointed. "May I come back another night?"

Instead of answering, Maleficent reached into her robe and pulled out another yellow flower. Once again, she blew on it, sending pollen into the air in front of

Aurora. And once again, Aurora's eyes fluttered shut and her body went limp.

As the other faeries looked on, Maleficent raised Aurora into the air. And then, in silence, they left the glen.

A short while later they arrived at the small cottage. Quietly, Maleficent floated Aurora into her room and gently lowered her onto her bed. Leaning over the princess, Maleficent felt a small smile tug at the corners of her lips. "Good night, beastie," she said gently before turning to go.

At the door, she paused to take one last look at Aurora. It hadn't been so bad after all to have her around the glen. But it was a one-time thing. It could never happen again. Ever.

CHAPTER SEVENTEEN

STEFAN LOOKED TERRIBLE. HE'D BEEN UP ALL NIGHT, PACING IN THE ROOM HE RARELY LEFT ANYMORE. THE SUN PEEKED OUT, MARKING THE DAWN OF ANOTHER DAY. If he hadn't been so distracted, perhaps this time of day would have reminded him of the daughter who had been named after it.

"You mock me," he murmured just as a servant entered the room behind him.

"Sire?" the servant questioned.

But Stefan did not turn, did not answer. He simply gazed ahead, not blinking.

The servant decided to go on with the news he'd been trusted with. "Majesty, your presence is requested by the queen."

"Leave me," Stefan said simply, acknowledging the servant's presence at last.

"Sire," the servant pleaded. "She is not well. The nurses are fearful that—"

"Leave me!" Stefan shouted. "Can you not see that I'm having a conversation?"

The servant stared at him, mystified. There was nobody else in the room. Clearly the king had come unhinged. The servant left, closing the door behind him, deciding to come back when the king was better rested. He only hoped it would not be too late. The queen had hours left at best. No one knew what disease plagued her, but most suspected she was dying of a broken heart.

Stefan had not even noticed that his wife was dying, just as he didn't notice that the servant had taken leave of him now. He started to walk straight ahead, still not blinking. "Intended to represent my triumph, my strength. And yet, day after day, year after year, you exist only to mock me. To remind me . . . It is not without purpose. Is it?"

He stared at the objects tormenting him: gigantic raven-black wings hanging in a glass case. Maleficent's wings. Shafts of morning light shone around them eerily.

Stefan moved up to the case, peering in. Then, resting his head on the glass, he whispered, "Is it?"

Suddenly, the wings flapped. Stefan jumped back, startled and alarmed. The wings were motionless once more. He took in a deep breath, unsuccessfully trying to calm his nerves.

"I spare her life and this is my reward? A curse upon my child? Upon my kingdom? Upon me?"

The wings flapped again, more powerfully this time.

Stefan continued his monologue. "When the curse fails, Maleficent will come for me. This I feel. This I know. As sure as the sun rises." He pointed an angry finger at the wings. "And on that day, I shall not be as benevolent. I will slay her as I should have done then. And I shall burn her carcass to ash!"

He paused, trying to catch his breath. He thought of the victory, of sweet vengeance. "And then . . . you will be once again a trophy. Nothing more."

The wings flapped angrily now, but Stefan just stared at them. Then, slowly, his face broke into a wide smile.

• • •

Maleficent's well-intended plans to keep Aurora away from the Moors quickly went awry. No sooner had she concluded that Aurora would never visit the Moors again than the beautiful princess found her way back to the Wall. And before Maleficent knew what she was doing, every night she was putting Aurora to sleep and bringing her into the faerie world.

In no time, Aurora had made herself at home amid the woods. And still worse, before Maleficent knew it, she was actually enjoying having the princess around.

There was something invigorating in the way the princess moved about the Moors in the star-filled nights. Whether she was hopping over a stream or wading through tall cattails, she was always reaching out, connecting herself to the world around her. And it wasn't just the flora she loved. She loved all the woodland creatures, too, from the beautiful dew faeries to the silly-looking hedgehog faeries, with their oversized ears and spiky backs.

And they *all* loved her. Even the jealous water faeries,

who were known to pull anyone they thought prettier into the water, admired Aurora's beauty. They would let her play along the water's edge, eager to show the princess the treasures of the streams. When they pulled out a shiny rock, Aurora would laugh in delight and praise them, causing the water faeries to blush with pride.

When they had no more stones to show Aurora, the water faeries would take to the top of the water, skating over its surface, leaving barely a ripple. Aurora would sit, entranced, as they put on a show for her, their long wings flowing out behind them. And when the show was over, they would dive under the water, leaving Aurora clapping on the shore.

The water faeries were not the only ones to vie for Aurora's attention. The grouchy wallerbogs loved to engage her in mud fights, which she inevitably lost. And even covered in mud, she kept smiling, thrilled to be part of this magical world. When she stumbled upon the more fearsome faeries, like the ram trolls, with their hunched shoulders, dark bark-like skin, and sharp branches that grew out of their arms and back, she didn't run but simply let them pass, aware that they too had a part in the way the Moors worked.

As the nights passed and Maleficent watched the princess, it became harder and harder to think of her as Stefan's daughter. She was nothing like him. While he had never respected nature, only ever seeing what the Moors could give to him, Aurora loved everything about the faerie world. She seemed instinctively to know how to be a part of it, and Maleficent found herself growing fond of the girl. Together they would wander, Aurora eagerly listening as Maleficent pointed out various plants and trees. And Maleficent found herself happy to listen as Aurora babbled on about whatever silly antics her aunts had been up to on that particular day. With each night, the pair grew more and more comfortable with each other. And while Maleficent had a hard time admitting it to herself, when she put a sleeping Aurora to bed as dawn broke, she was sad to leave her.

In Aurora, Maleficent had found a kindred spirit. Someone whom she could teach and someone from whom she could learn. Aurora's heart was wide open, eager to love, while Maleficent's was still closed up tight. Yet seeing how free and happy Aurora was, Maleficent couldn't help wondering if perhaps she had been doing herself a disservice all that time by being so cold. Even in the short time that Aurora had been a part of the Moors, Maleficent had felt a thawing toward her from the creatures who had ignored her before the girl's arrival. Through Aurora, they began to see a softer side of Maleficent. And Maleficent couldn't help enjoying being part of the bigger community once again.

But despite how much Maleficent liked having Aurora around, there was a heavy weight on her shoulders. She knew the visits would have to end. *They* have *to end,* she reminded herself on many occasions, *because of* my *curse.*

"Why can't I ever come here during the day?" Aurora asked Maleficent one night as the pair wandered through Snow Faeries Meadow. All around them, the iridescent faeries, their wings imprinted with unique snowflake shapes, flitted over the pond in the center of the meadow or played around a big old tree that dominated the shore. From where Aurora and Maleficent stood, the snow faeries looked like hundreds of bright lights that illuminated the tree and made it glow.

Maleficent looked down at the girl, unsure of what to say. She couldn't tell her the truth: that if her "aunts" discovered where she was and with whom she was spending her time, they would be very, very upset. Nor could she tell her the reason they would be so upset: that Maleficent was not what she seemed. So instead, she simply said, "It is the only time the Wall is open to you."

Before the girl could ask any more questions, Maleficent strode on, forcing Aurora to run to keep up. But through the rest of that night and into the next few days, Aurora's question tugged at Maleficent. She wanted to see Aurora playing in the Moors during the day. If she was being honest, she wanted to see Aurora all the time and, preferably, for many years. But for that to happen, she would have to do something about the curse. . . .

One night, weeks after Aurora's first trip to the

Moors and only a few weeks before her sixteenth birthday, Maleficent lay Aurora down in her bed. And as she
had done every night for many nights, she pulled the
covers up gently and whispered, "Good night, beastie."
But on this particular evening, as the moon began to
sink into the horizon and the sun began to rise, she
softly added, "I retract my curse. Let it be no more."

As the words left her mouth, the room filled with
magic. The air crackled and shimmered and a gentle
wind rustled. But the magic didn't touch Aurora. Narrowing her eyes, Maleficent stepped closer and repeated
the words, this time more forcefully. "I retract my curse.
Let it be no more."

Once again, magic filled the air and the room shimmered. But once again, the magic flowed around Aurora,
leaving her untouched.

Feeling dread begin to build in the pit of her stomach, Maleficent spoke the words again, with still more
passion. And then she repeated them. Again, and again,
and again she spoke, mustering all her strength and willing all her magic to break the curse. The room began to

shake as the massive amount of magic collected in the small space, but Maleficent went on, oblivious. All she could see was Aurora, sleeping the way she would forever if the curse could not be broken. Letting out one last cry, she threw her staff in the air and sent a huge burst of magic raining down over the room.

But it still didn't touch Aurora.

Lowering her staff, Maleficent slowly left the room, her heart aching. She had done everything she could. Yet the curse, the one she had so foolishly called a gift, could not be undone. Which meant, one way or another, in a few short weeks, Aurora would prick her finger on a spinning wheel and never wake up.

CHAPTER EIGHTEEN

FILLED WITH REGRET, MALEFICENT
SPENT THE NEXT DAY SITTING LIST-
LESSLY BY THE WALL. THE THOUGHT
OF SEEING AURORA'S INNOCENT FACE
THAT EVENING WAS HEART-WRENCHING. She felt this
new, intense need to protect the girl from the ugliness of
the world, but ironically, she was part of it. For she was
the one who had cursed her, and she was the one who
had made it impossible for her to live a full life, on the
Moors or with her family. And, Maleficent thought with
a sad laugh, Aurora had been the one to remind her just
how important family and friends were. Aurora's birthday was swiftly approaching, and Maleficent felt more
hopeless, more powerless with every day that passed.

By the time Aurora arrived that night, Maleficent
was overtaken by feelings she had thought she had left
behind. But never one to show her pain or fear, she

simply remained quiet, the torment on her face the only indication of what was going on inside her head.

Unaware of what her faerie godmother was going through, Aurora prattled on about the cake she had made that day. She had had to go far to find the berries, but it had been worth it, she said, as the aunts were very fond of sweets. Distracted by a faerie fluttering between trees, its green body mimicking the leaves, Aurora interrupted herself, asking, "Do all of the Fair People have wings?"

"Most do," Maleficent replied shortly, not in the mood for conversation. It was hard enough just listening to Aurora's singsong voice without breaking down, admitting that she had cursed her, and then begging for forgiveness.

But Aurora didn't take the hint. "Then why don't you?"

"It's not anything I wish to talk about," Maleficent said softly.

"I'm just curious because all the other faeries have wings and—"

It was too much for Maleficent. "Enough!" she snapped.

Aurora instantly became quiet and they walked on in silence. Glancing at the princess, Maleficent saw that her face had grown pale and her eyes were watery. Seeing the pain she had caused, Maleficent softened. "I had wings once," she said, her voice barely a whisper, the pain sharp just from remembering them. "But they were stolen from me. And that's all I'll say about it."

But she had given Aurora only a tidbit of information and the princess wanted more. "What color were they?" she asked, growing excited. "How big were they?"

Looking off into the distance, as though she could see them on the horizon, Maleficent smiled sadly. "So big they dragged behind me when I walked. And they were strong." As she spoke of her long-lost wings, she felt an itch on her back where the scars remained. "They could carry me above the clouds and straight into headwinds. They never faltered. Not even once. I could trust them."

As her words faded, Maleficent dared not look at

Aurora. She had never said those words aloud. Never admitted to anyone just how much the wings had meant to her and how much it had hurt when Stefan took them away. They had reminded her of her mother, but they had also become the features that she linked to her own identity—her soaring, organic identity.

Suddenly, she felt long fingers intertwine with hers. Looking down, she saw that Aurora had put her delicate hand in hers and was squeezing tight. Meeting her gaze, Maleficent saw the pain she felt reflected in Aurora's eyes. It overwhelmed her. Slowly, she pulled her hand free. She had already lost so much she loved. And now it was only a matter of time before Aurora, too, was taken away.

• • •

Maleficent's wings were carrying him, higher and higher into a sky the color of soot. He struggled against them, kicking wildly. Soon he saw their target. The Thorn Wall gleamed in the moonlight below him, the boulder-sized thorns pointed up. The wings were taking him right above it. Even if he survived the fall, he would never survive the impalement he was sure to experience. Just as he felt the wings let go, Stefan woke up, gasping, in his chamber.

Another nightmare. Would those wings never cease haunting him, even in sleep? Quickly, he got dressed and headed to the battlements. He needed to be active, to see the progress his men were making.

But as Stefan approached the scene, he was sorely disappointed. Nothing was being done. There were no workers in sight besides the overseer of the ironworkers, who was snoring loudly in the corner. Stefan grabbed a bucket of water and threw it at the sleeping man. The overseer bolted up, shocked and disheveled.

"Where are your men?" Stefan asked.

"In their beds, Majesty," the overseer responded, shivering.

"Get them back to work without delay."

The man hesitated, unsure how to refuse the king. "They're exhausted, sire. But I'll have them back to work at first light."

"I need them back to work now," Stefan insisted.

The overseer wasn't sure what the king meant. Work now? "It's the wee hours," he started.

"Aye, aye," the king agreed. "It is the wee hours. So wake them up."

"Sire?"

His patience exhausted, Stefan slammed the man against the wall. "So wake them up and get them back to work now! We're running out of time. *Go now!*"

For the next few days, Maleficent walked around in a conflicted daze. She barely spoke, didn't eat, and didn't even bother tricking the pixies or turning Diaval into various animals. Even being in her grove or running her hands over the velvety cattails gave her little comfort. More and more often she found herself making her way to the shores of the Dark Pond. On the edge of the Moors farthest from the Wall, the pond was home to the darker creatures of the faerie world. It was there the ram trolls resided alongside hog trolls with their furry hog-wart mounts. The pond itself was dark, too.

No wallerbogs cleaned its waters, and the stone faeries dared not go close. It was a lonely place. A place for the dark-hearted. *It is where I deserve to be,* Maleficent told herself every time she arrived. *For only someone with a heart as dark as mine could do something so evil to a girl with a heart as light as Aurora's.*

Aware of his mistress's dark thoughts, Diaval often accompanied her to the Dark Pond, where he would sit silently with her until she was ready to leave. But one afternoon, several days after Aurora had taken Maleficent's hand in hers, Diaval was not there when Maleficent left the grove. Discovering her gone, he quickly flew to the Dark Pond and, upon arriving, landed on her shoulder. He began to rub his feathered head against her as though comforting her. But Maleficent was not in the mood. "Stop!" she ordered.

He began to rub harder. With an angry wave of her hand, she transformed him into a man. When he was up on two feet, he looked at Maleficent, his expression worried. "Mistress," he said, "you're miserable."

"I'm perfectly fine," she replied.

"No, you're miserable," Diaval repeated.

"I'm going to make *you* miserable if you don't stop saying that."

Diaval shook his head. There was no getting through to her with words. But maybe . . . ? He slowly reached out a hand and touched her shoulder, hoping to comfort the upset faerie. It didn't work. She turned her icy glare on him and shook his hand off. As Maleficent turned and began to walk away, she silently fumed. What right did Diaval have to try to comfort her? Who did he think he was? He was why she was in this mess in the first place. If he hadn't been so bent on making sure Aurora was all right in that little cottage with those obnoxious faeries, she never would have seen the child. Never would have watched her grow up. Never would have grown fond of her. Never would have had to tell her something that was going to break the girl's heart. But that was what she had to do. Maleficent knew that now. It was what had been eating away at her since she'd last seen Aurora. She had to tell her the truth about the world. And it wasn't going to be easy. Letting out a groan, she stalked to the Wall to wait for night, when the stars and the truth would all come out.

A light snow had fallen during the day so that now, as Maleficent and Aurora walked across the Moors and made their way to one of their favorite spots, the Snow Faerie Meadow, their footsteps were muffled by the soft powder. In the cold they could see their breath coming out in little clouds. The landscape was beautiful, the hills covered in white and the stars twinkling in the sky above.

If only I didn't have to ruin the beauty with darkness, Maleficent thought. Straightening her shoulders, she shook off the thought. It was now or never.

"Aurora," she began, "there is something I need to tell you."

"Yes?" Aurora said, looking up at her, innocent and pure as ever.

Maleficent stopped walking and shuffled on her feet for a moment, unsure how to proceed. "There is evil in the world," she finally said. "I cannot keep you safe from it."

Expecting the princess to look scared, Maleficent was surprised to see her smile. "I'm almost sixteen, Godmother. I can take care of myself."

Maleficent smiled despite herself. The girl was so brave yet so naive. "I understand. But that's not—"

Aurora interrupted her. "I have a plan," she said, her face lighting up with excitement. "When I'm older, I'm going to live here in the Moors with you. And then we can look after each other."

Looking at the proud smile on Aurora's face, Maleficent had no choice but to smile back. It was clear the girl had put a lot of thought into this. And that she not only wanted to live in the Moors but wanted to be a part of Maleficent's life was beyond touching. Aurora didn't know what her future held, the curse that was inevitable. She thought she had her whole life in front of her. And she wanted to spend it in the Moors, not in the cottage with her aunts, where things would be easier. There she had a home and was surrounded by family—at least, she thought they were family. There in the Moors, she would have only the woodland creatures as companions. True, she would also have Diaval and Maleficent, but what fun could they possibly be after any length of time? But it would be so nice. . . .

As Aurora's words sank in, Maleficent's heart began to beat faster. *Wait a minute,* she thought. *Why didn't I think of it sooner?* Maybe, just maybe, there was a way to prevent the curse and give Aurora what she wanted—and, frankly, what Maleficent wanted, too. If the girl lived in the Moors, she would never be able to touch a spinning wheel. She could avoid the fate placed upon her nearly sixteen years earlier. Her excitement building, Maleficent turned to Aurora. "You don't have to wait until you're older," she said. "You could live here now."

But Aurora shook her head sadly. "My aunts would never let me."

"I thought you could take care of yourself," Maleficent said, hoping she didn't sound as desperate as she felt. Now that the idea had lodged itself in her brain, she couldn't let it go.

"I can," Aurora said. "But they would be sad without me." She paused and then smiled as she, too, had an idea. "Could they come visit me?"

Maleficent stifled a groan. Knotgrass, Thistlewit, and Flittle? Here? The pixie traitors back in the Moors and, worse still, in her grove? The idea was abhorrent. The three little pixies had abandoned their home to live with the enemy . . . and yet they *had* raised Aurora. And while it pained Maleficent to admit it, they hadn't done that bad a job. Even if it had taken a little unseen help from her and Diaval. Looking down at the hopeful expression on Aurora's face, Maleficent knew she had no choice. If she wanted the girl to be safe in the Moors, she was going to have to let the pixies through the Wall. Though it wouldn't be all the time. Just every once in a while. But that was something she and Aurora could discuss at a later point. For now, she was simply going to say yes.

Aurora let out a happy squeal and clapped her hands. "Then I will!" she exclaimed. "I'll sleep in a tree and eat berries and black nuts, and all the Fair People will be my friends. I'll be happy here for the rest of my life. I'm going to tell them tomorrow." As she spoke, she skipped ahead, lost in thoughts of her life to come.

Behind her, Maleficent watched, pleased that things were going to work out after all.

CHAPTER NINETEEN

AFTER TUCKING AURORA SAFELY INTO HER BED, MALEFICENT SPENT THE REMAINDER OF THE NIGHT WANDERING RESTLESSLY THROUGH THE WOODS NEAR THE COTTAGE. THE NEXT DAY WAS IMPORTANT FOR SO MANY REASONS. In only three days' time, Aurora would be sixteen. And before that day arrived, she needed to come to the Moors. While Maleficent trusted Aurora to stay strong and stand up to her "aunts," she wanted to be nearby in case. And with Aurora's sixteenth birthday fast approaching, she felt an even greater sense of urgency. Aurora needed to be in the Moors—and safe from spinning wheels—immediately.

As the sun rose, Diaval joined Maleficent and the two made their way to the clearing. From the safety of the trees, they watched as life began to stir in the cottage. They heard the clink of pans being put on the stove and the sizzle as eggs were cooked. That was followed by the sounds of dishes being cleaned and the squabbling of the three pixies over who had left the dishes overnight. Maleficent smiled. It would be good for Aurora to get away from those three, even if they did have to visit occasionally.

Finally, Aurora appeared at the cottage door. Looking up at the cloudless blue sky, she smiled and, after saying a quick good-bye to her aunts, began to walk into the woods as she was wont to do every morning. But that morning was different. Because on that morning, not only was she being followed by Maleficent and Diaval, she was gathering up the courage to tell her aunts the news.

"Aunties," Maleficent heard her say as the girl walked along. "I'm almost sixteen and I need a life of my own." Maleficent smiled as she listened to Aurora practice her speech. "I love you very much but it's time—"

Her voice cut off abruptly as she heard a noise in the bushes. Looking about, she saw a wide tree and ducked behind it. Maleficent had heard the noise, too, and turned her head toward the nearby bushes. A moment later, she watched as a handsome young man stepped out, leading a large white horse. He pushed a strand of thick brown hair out of his brown eyes and looked around.

"Is someone there?" the young man called out.

From her hiding spot, Aurora peeked out. Seeing the man, she quickly ducked back, her cheeks turning red.

Seeing Aurora's reaction, Maleficent was filled with an ominous feeling. The princess had never seen a man up close before, let alone one this handsome. And there was no denying it: the young man was very, very handsome. He had a regal way of carrying himself and broad shoulders that tapered into a narrow waist, and from what she could see of them, his eyes looked kind. What would happen if he and Aurora spoke? Would he enchant her the way Stefan had enchanted Maleficent all those years before? Would she still want to live in the Moors? Or would she betray the faerie world like her father before her?

As those thoughts raced through Maleficent's mind,

the young man took another step closer. "Hello," he called out toward where Aurora hid.

Cautiously, Aurora stepped out. "Sorry to bother you," he said. "But I'm on my way to King Stefan's castle and I've become hopelessly lost. Can you help me?" As he spoke, he took another step forward.

Nervous, Aurora stepped back, stumbling over a rock and falling to the ground with a thump.

"I'm sorry," the young man said. "That was my doing. I rushed in too fast and frightened you. Forgive me?" He held out his hand to help her up.

Just as he pulled her to her feet, a ray of sun shot down, turning Aurora's golden hair still more golden and illuminating her tall, lean body and beautiful face. Maleficent watched as the young man's eyes grew wide. He was entranced. She saw his breath quicken and his face flush. She also saw that Aurora's hand nervously went to her throat, as though she was unsure of herself in front of the man.

"It's that way," she finally said, her voice breathless.

The young man nodded but didn't answer.

"The castle," Aurora added, worried that he didn't know what she was talking about.

He nodded again.

Watching, Maleficent didn't know whether to laugh or cry. The young man was clearly love struck. And Aurora? Well, she was growing bolder, less shy, with each passing moment. If it weren't so upsetting, Maleficent would be proud of her brave Aurora. But selfishly, she wanted the girl to stay quiet.

"What's your name?" Aurora asked, trying to get him to speak.

The young man once again didn't say anything. Not for a moment. He just stood there, transfixed and seemingly unable to think of his own name. Finally, he shook his head and blinked, as if coming to from a long sleep. "Phillip," he said. "It's Phillip."

Aurora smiled. "Hello, Phillip."

"What's yours?" Phillip asked, mesmerized.

"Aurora."

"Hello, Aurora," he said softly.

As around them the birds chirped and the wind blew

gently, the pair stood there, gazing into each other's eyes. For them, it was as though time were standing still. For Maleficent, it was as though time were speeding up. She could clearly see what was to happen. This Phillip would woo her Aurora. Take her away and never be able to protect her from the curse. And Aurora would go, unaware of the danger she faced. With a sigh, Maleficent waited to see if she was right.

"Well, thank you for your help," Phillip said, finally breaking the silence. "I'd best be off, then." He whistled loudly and his white horse trotted over. Phillip pulled himself into the saddle and reluctantly turned to go.

"Will you be back?" Aurora called out.

Smiling, Phillip looked over his shoulder. "Nothing could stop me."

Letting out a happy laugh, Aurora said, "Then I'll see you soon. Good-bye, Phillip." She waved as he rode off, looking back over his shoulder as if to make sure she was still there.

Long after Phillip had disappeared over the horizon, Aurora stood there, until, humming a happy little tune, she left the glen. In the woods nearby, Maleficent fretted. Diaval, who had been sitting on her shoulder the whole time, began to pick incessantly at her with his beak. Reaching up, she grabbed his bird feet. "Stop doing that!" she hissed. When he began to squirm, Maleficent waved a hand, transforming him into his human form.

"That boy is the answer!" Diaval said the instant he could speak.

Maleficent shook her head. "No, Diaval," she said sadly.

"Yes!" he countered. "True Love's Kiss, remember? It will break the spell!"

"True Love's Kiss?" Maleficent repeated. Was he serious? Did he really not get it? This was why she had wanted to keep Aurora in the Moors in the first place. Because there were fools who might actually believe there was a way to stop the inevitable. But there wasn't. There could never be. She knew the truth all too well, as she had lived it herself. Filled with renewed bitterness, she went on. "Have you not worked it out yet? I cursed her that way because there is no such thing."

Diaval didn't say anything for a moment. Then, softly, he said, "That may be the way *you* feel. But what about Aurora? That boy could be her only chance. It's *her* fate, not yours! Haven't you done enough?"

The words cut deep. What Diaval said was true. She had already done enough, too much. She had put Aurora in this position, yet . . . it made her furious that Diaval had to point it out. He knew nothing! What right did he have to make her feel worse than she already did? Her temper flaring, she lifted her hand, ready to transform him. But Diaval spoke, surprising her.

"Go ahead!" he cried. "Turn me into whatever you want. A bird, a worm. I don't care anymore." Not waiting to see what she would do, Diaval turned and walked away.

Behind him, Maleficent watched him go, her emotions churning. She hated him for talking to her like that. Hated him for making her feel guilty. Yet if she hated him so much, why was she so upset to see him go? Maleficent sighed. Why had everything gotten so complicated?

CHAPTER TWENTY

MALEFICENT WAS ABOUT TO FIND OUT THAT THINGS HAD INDEED GOTTEN MUCH, MUCH MORE COMPLICATED. IN THE LITTLE COTTAGE IN THE CLEAR- ING, AURORA AWOKE ON THE DAY BEFORE HER BIRTHDAY IN THE BEST OF MOODS. She had met the most handsome man, was going to live in the Moors, and, best yet, would get to spend more time with her faerie godmother. The only thing that gave her pause was that she needed to tell her aunts she was leaving. That part dampened her mood slightly. After all, the three of them had raised her when her parents had died, and while they could be a little odd, she loved each one of them. Sighing, she got out of bed. It was time.

Walking into the cottage's main room, she smiled when she saw her aunts bickering once again. Hear- ing her footsteps, they all froze, then turned toward her, looking oddly guilty. But Aurora ignored that and plunged ahead with her news. "I need to talk to you about something," she began.

"Anything, lovie," Flittle said, straightening out her hair, which was a tad disheveled.

"I'm sorry to have to tell you this, and please don't be sad, but I'll be sixteen tomorrow and so . . ."

Her voice trailed off as she struggled to go on. "Yes?" Thistlewit prompted.

Aurora took a deep breath, and then in a rush, her words running into one another, she said, "I'm leaving home."

Expecting tears and sadness, she was surprised when Knotgrass's face turned red with anger. "Oh, no you aren't!" she cried. "I didn't suffer all these years in this miserable hovel with those two imbeciles so you would ruin it on the last day! We are taking you back to your father—" As the last words left her lips, Knotgrass slapped her hand over her mouth. She hadn't meant to say that.

Aurora's face grew pale. "My father?" she repeated. "You told me my parents were dead."

The three aunts looked at one another, silently figuring out what to do. Finally, Flittle patted the bench next to her. "You'd better sit down," she said.

Confused, Aurora did as she was told and listened as they began their story.

"Faerie Godmother!"

Aurora's voice rang out through the glen. Hearing the panic in her voice, Maleficent emerged from the shadows while Diaval hung back. It was the day before Aurora's sixteenth birthday, and she was supposed to have come after telling her aunts that she was leaving. Clearly, something had happened, and knowing the three pixies and their conniving ways to stay on Stefan's good side, Maleficent figured they must have told Aurora about her past to try to keep her with them. But just how much had they said?

"I'm here," Maleficent said, glancing at the princess.

The girl's usually bright eyes were full of tears and her hair was a mess, as though she had been pulling at it incessantly. Maleficent waited, fearing what Aurora was about to say.

"When were you going to tell me that I'm cursed?" she asked, her voice full of pain.

Maleficent had been right. Those meddlesome faeries-in-waiting *had* told Aurora what had happened years earlier. But Aurora had said only that she had been cursed. She hadn't said *who* had cursed her. . . .

"*Well?* Is it true?" Aurora asked, her voice pleading.

Maleficent nodded. "It is," she said simply.

Aurora's face fell. "I was just a baby!" she cried. "Who would do such a terrible thing to a baby?" Her big blue eyes met Maleficent's. "My aunts said it was an evil faerie. They said her name. They said . . . they said . . ." She choked on her sobs, unable to say the name out loud.

Seeing the hurt this moment was causing her, Maleficent couldn't stand it any longer. Turning away so as not to meet Aurora's gaze, she said the name aloud. "Maleficent."

Behind her, Aurora's eyes grew wide as something clicked and she began to put the pieces of the puzzle together. "Is that *your* name?" she asked. "Are *you* Maleficent? Are *you* the one who cursed me?"

Slowly, Maleficent turned to face the princess. This was not the way she had wanted Aurora to find out who she was and what she had done. But what else could she do? The truth was going to come out one way or another. "Yes," she said softly.

Aurora's hand went to her heart as the reality of Maleficent's confession hit her like an arrow. She stared at her, as though seeing Maleficent for the first time. The gaze burned Maleficent. She had just turned Aurora's world upside down. She had done the same thing Stefan had done to her, made the princess trust in her and then broken that trust cruelly. *Such irony,* Maleficent thought as Aurora began to back away. "Wait!" Maleficent cried, reaching out a hand.

Aurora reared back from the touch, shaking her head. "No!" she cried. "Don't touch me! *You're* the evil that's in the world! It's you!" Aurora turned and raced off, disappearing into the woods.

Watching her go, Maleficent felt all the strength drain out of her. It was hard for her to breathe. She had spent so long denying what she had done, to herself and to Aurora. And now she was being punished.

She stood there for a long while, wishing she had the power to go back in time and never utter the curse in the first place. Never mention a spinning wheel or True Love's Kiss . . . Suddenly, she felt a flash of hope. Perhaps there was still a way to make things right. Perhaps Diaval had been right and true love could exist for some people. Raising her eyes, she met the raven's gaze. "Find the boy," she said.

As Diaval flew into the air, Maleficent said a silent prayer that she wasn't too late.

CHAPTER TWENTY-ONE

MALEFICENT SLOWLY AND SADLY MADE HER WAY BACK TO THE GLEN. WHILE SHE WASN'T THERE TO WITNESS IT, SHE KNEW EXACTLY WHAT AURORA WAS GOING TO DO NEXT. SHE WAS GOING TO RACE HOME, GRAB THE HORSE FROM THE COTTAGE'S SMALL STABLE, AND TAKE OFF. She would gallop furiously out of the woods and onto the road that took her straight to the castle. She wouldn't stop to think about what her aunts would say when they found her gone. She wouldn't stop to think about why Maleficent would have lied to her. She wouldn't even stop to think about what her father would say when she arrived at the castle gates. She would just ride, tears streaming down her face.

She *would* think about the fact that she had a father. And a mother. And that she was a princess. Those things she would think about. A lot. So by the time she arrived at the castle, some of her anger would have been replaced by anticipation. For she was going to meet her family.

And while Maleficent wasn't there to witness the reunion, she had a good idea of how that would go, too. King Stefan would see Aurora, and at first he would think she was just some common country girl. After all, he, more focused on Maleficent and his own selfish fear, hadn't really thought about her in years, and she most definitely didn't wear royal clothes. Then, when she told him she was his daughter and tried to hug him, he would hold her at arm's length, trying to see if she was really, truly his flesh and blood. When he decided she was, he would soften, just a bit. Maleficent hated to think of him softening, but she had to believe he had *some* heart left under all that paranoia and armor.

Then, Maleficent figured, he would tell Aurora that she was beautiful, like her mother. But that would be as far as his fatherly kindness would go. For he would quickly realize that Aurora had arrived back a day early and that the faeries had not done their job. He would realize what that meant: that the curse could still be inflicted on his newly returned daughter. He would panic and order that Aurora be brought to a safe place, where she would be forced to remain until the next day. Aurora wouldn't have a chance to argue, but before she was led away, she *would* ask about her mother. And Stefan would ignore her question, leaving it to a hapless guard to break the news that had spread throughout the kingdom: that her mother had died.

That was the way it would happen, Maleficent mused as she sat in her grove, the light fading around her. Suddenly, she sat up straighter. It didn't *have* to happen that way, though. Not if she could get to the cottage before Aurora took off and try to convince her to stay.

She jumped up, raced over the Moors, passed through the Wall, and made her way to the clearing in the woods. Bursting into Aurora's bedroom, she found it empty. Her eyes narrowed. "Those fools!" she shouted. They hadn't stopped her! How could they have let her go when what waited at the castle would surely hurt her?

Hearing Diaval's caw, Maleficent turned and saw him perched in the window. Waving her hand, she transformed him into a man and waited for his report. "I found the boy," he said.

Maleficent nodded. "Show me," she ordered.

Together, the two made their way out of the cottage and into the woods. They didn't have to go far. Phillip was nearby, heading toward the cottage in hopes of seeing Aurora again.

Stepping forward, Maleficent saw Phillip take in her horns and long dark cloak and pale slightly. But he didn't step back. Instead, he put his hand on his sword and met Maleficent's gaze head-on. Despite herself, Maleficent was impressed. "I'm looking for a girl," he said.

"Of course you are," she replied.

Phillip was about to ask just how the horned woman knew that when Maleficent pulled out a yellow flower and blew its pollen toward him. In moments, he was asleep. That taken care of, Maleficent looked around. Now she needed a quick way to reach the castle. "I need a horse." Her eyes landed on Diaval perched in a tree. She smiled. That could work quite well.

Moments later, as the sun began to sink below the horizon, Maleficent galloped down the road on the back of a beautiful jet-black horse. She held a sleeping Phillip in front of her as they traveled toward the castle. With each big stride of the Diaval horse, they grew closer and closer. And with each big stride, Maleficent grew more and more worried. The sun was almost down. Time was running out . . . fast.

As Maleficent raced toward Aurora, she felt the presence of the girl growing stronger. All their time together had created an invisible, magical link between the pair. It allowed Maleficent to sense where Aurora was and how she was feeling. At that moment, she could almost see Aurora in her room in the castle, pacing back and forth before the door. She wouldn't be happy that she had come all that way just to be locked up like some prisoner. So when a handmaiden knocked at the door,

Aurora would eagerly open it. She would ignore the other girl when she said something ignorant like "This room is for the princess when she arrives. No one should be occupying it." Aurora would see her chance and, not bothering to correct the handmaiden, would push past her and run out. Turning a corner, she would slow her pace. And that was when she would feel it for the first time—a strange ache in the tip of her finger. An ache that she desperately wanted to make go away. She wouldn't be able to explain it, and her feet would continue moving toward an unknown destination.

On the road outside the castle, Maleficent felt the ache in her finger as well. But unlike Aurora, she knew what it meant. It meant that the curse was growing stronger as the time for it to be fulfilled approached. And until that time came, Aurora would make her way through the entire castle looking for the one thing that would take away the pain—a spinning wheel. She would enter the laundry room, with its long mending table, but move on when she saw only needles and thread. Her finger throbbing more than ever, she would keep going, desperate to find what she was looking for, but still not able to put a name to it. Knowing that all this was happening, Maleficent squeezed her legs, urging Diaval on faster.

A few minutes later, they arrived at the outskirts of the kingdom. Cresting a hill, Diaval reared up as the large ominous structure came into view. This was the first time Maleficent had seen the castle in nearly sixteen years. And it was no longer the beautiful castle it had once been. The blue stone had been covered entirely by iron, making the walls impenetrable. Nasty-looking iron spikes topped the parapets and towers, and along the ramparts, soldiers in iron armor paced back and forth holding iron weapons. King Stefan had done everything in his power to make his castle Maleficent-proof. Now, looking up at it, Maleficent realized he had done his job thoroughly. It was going to be nearly impossible for her to get inside. But nearly impossible and impossible were two very different things, and she wasn't willing to give up yet. Plus, even if she couldn't get in, Phillip could. And that was all she needed.

Just then, Maleficent felt a cooling in the air. With a feeling of dread, she turned and looked toward the horizon in the west. Time had run out. As she watched, the sun sank lower and lower into the horizon, the last rays spreading their weak warmth across the countryside. And then, just as the rays faded and disappeared altogether, Maleficent felt it. A pain deep inside her that built and built and then burst, causing her to cry out.

"It's done," she said, her voice aching. The curse had been fulfilled. Somewhere inside that iron fortress, Aurora had found a spinning wheel and pricked her finger on it. And somewhere in there, she now lay in a sleep that would last forever. Unless . . . Maleficent looked down at Phillip. Kicking Diaval on, she raced toward the castle, holding Aurora's last hope carefully in front of her.

CHAPTER TWENTY-TWO

NIGHT HAD FALLEN. HOURS HAD PASSED SINCE MALEFICENT HAD FELT THE PAIN IN HER FINGER AND KNOWN AURORA WAS LOST TO SLEEP. NOW, STANDING IN FRONT OF KING STEFAN'S CASTLE, MALEFICENT AND DIAVAL, ONCE MORE IN HIS HUMAN FORM, STARED UP AT THE BIG IRON GATES. Behind them, Phillip slept on, propped up against a tree. The gates were unguarded and oddly quiet. Noticing that, Maleficent cocked her head. On one hand, that was good news, as it meant Maleficent could enter the castle undetected. But on the other hand, it meant she had no idea what to expect once inside.

"He's waiting for you in there," Diaval pointed out. He didn't bother to say who, as Maleficent knew all too well. "If we go inside those walls, we'll never get out alive."

Maleficent continued to stare straight ahead, barely registering Diaval's words. "Then don't come," she said absently. "It's not your fight." Using her staff, she lifted the sleeping Phillip and began to move on.

Behind her, Diaval let out a sigh. Once, just once, it would be nice if Maleficent were able to see what was really going on. It would be nice to hear her say, "Please come with me, Diaval. We can do anything as long as we're together." But Diaval knew those were words he would never hear. And while he wished it were different, he also knew he could never let Maleficent go into that castle alone. Letting out a little groan, he ran to catch up.

Inside the castle, the halls were quiet. News that the curse had been fulfilled had spread like wildfire, and servants and soldiers alike quaked with fear at King Stefan's rage. He had already taken his anger out on the three dimwitted pixies who had let Aurora come back too early. After berating them for hours, calling them useless and failures, he had ordered them to find someone—anyone—who could give his daughter the kiss of true love.

What he didn't know was that his own first love was now inside his castle, making her way closer with the one man who might stand a chance at waking up his daughter.

As soon as Maleficent had passed through the castle's main gate, she had felt the weight of the iron on her. While she was able to avoid touching it, the dark metal was everywhere. It lined the walls, carefully sculpted into the shape of brambles and thorns, effectively making it appear like an iron version of her Thorn Wall. The iron thorns thrust out of the wall and jutted down from the ceiling, forcing Maleficent to walk carefully and keep her pace slow. Eager to get to Aurora, she chafed at the speed. But when they heard a guard approaching and had to duck back into the shadows, Maleficent realized that walking was not as bad as the searing pain she felt when the iron touched her back.

When the guard had finally passed and the coast was clear, Maleficent stepped away from the wall, gasping for breath.

"Are you burned?" Diaval asked, concern lacing his voice.

But Maleficent didn't answer. Gritting her teeth, she simply said, "Carry on."

For the next few minutes, they walked along in silence. Hearing still more footsteps, they once again hid in the shadows. But this time Maleficent was careful to keep her back off the walls. Peeking out, she saw that the footsteps belonged to two handmaidens. They carried clean linens in their arms as they scurried down the hall.

"How long will she sleep?" one of them asked.

The other shrugged. "Forever, I guess."

Maleficent looked at Diaval and raised an eyebrow. The women could be talking about only one person: Aurora. Maleficent waited until the pair had moved past, then silently slipped back into the hall. Diaval joined her, holding Phillip up in his arms. They began to follow the handmaidens.

A short while later they arrived at the princess's room. They ducked behind a thick set of drapes that covered the wall opposite the room, and Maleficent took stock of the situation. Two soldiers stood guard, and through the open door, Maleficent could hear the grating voices of Knotgrass, Thistlewit, and Flittle. The trio seemed to be in the middle of forcing someone to kiss the princess.

"This is Princess Aurora," Maleficent heard Knotgrass say.

"Isn't she beautiful?" Flittle added.

A male voice answered, "Yes."

Then Knotgrass spoke again. "Are you in love with her?"

Hidden behind the drapes, Maleficent rolled her eyes. Did those three nincompoops honestly think that all it would take was some stranger saying he loved the princess and kissing her for the curse to lift? Poof? Just like that? Beside her, Diaval saw her expression and smiled knowingly. While they didn't irk him as much as they did Maleficent, he was well aware of how silly the three pixies could be, and he sympathized.

When the young man in the room replied that he was "madly" in love with Aurora, Maleficent heard Knotgrass say, "You may kiss her, then."

There was a moment of silence and Maleficent knew that the young man was kissing Aurora. There was another moment as everyone in the room waited for Aurora to wake up. But of course, she didn't.

If she hadn't been so distraught, Maleficent would have laughed out loud when she heard one of the pixies stamp her feet in frustration. She did love when they got worked up. Then Flittle cried out, "If it was true love, you would have woken her!"

"I'll try again," Maleficent heard the young man say.

But the pixies wanted him out. A moment later he appeared in the doorway, looking dejected. Behind him, Thistlewit and Flittle stood in the door, their arms folded across their chests. They waited for him to walk away before turning to the two handmaidens, who had been waiting patiently. Reaching out, the pixies snatched the linens and, with a huff, turned and closed the door behind them. The two handmaidens looked at each other and then, shrugging, turned and walked down the hall. Within moments, the hall was once again empty save for the two guards and the threesome hidden behind the curtain.

Maleficent knew this was her chance. Moving slightly away from the curtain, she waved her hand in front of Phillip and softly whispered, "Wake." Then, with a gentle shove, she pushed him out from behind the curtain. He stumbled into the hall, the noise alerting the guards, who quickly raised their swords, unsure where the young man had come from. At the same moment, the door opened and the three pixies bustled out, nearly crashing into Phillip.

Looking around, Phillip shook his head, as though trying to clear his vision. "Pardon me," he said, seeing the three pixies. "I'm embarrassed to say I don't know where I am." Despite having just woken up from a magical sleep and not knowing where he was or how he had gotten there, he looked every part the perfect, handsome gentleman, Maleficent had to admit.

The faeries must have thought so, too, because they didn't slam the door in his face. Instead, they informed him that he was in King Stefan's castle.

Upon hearing that, Phillip looked surprised. "This is where I'm meant to be," he said, trying to understand. "Odd that I can't recall how I got here. My father sent me to see the king."

Knotgrass perked up. If his father had sent him to see the king, perhaps this young man was someone of importance. There was one way to find out. "Who is your father?" she asked.

"King John of Ulstead," Phillip replied.

The three faeries exchanged looks as they mouthed, "Prince." Without a word of explanation, they pulled him into the room.

In the hall, Maleficent anxiously waited, straining to hear what was going on. While she had been surprised to hear Phillip say his father was a king, she was rather pleased. It seemed only right that if Aurora, a princess, were to be awoken, it would be by the kiss of true love from a prince.

"What's your name?" she heard Knotgrass ask, followed by the sound of footsteps as the group made their way toward Aurora.

"Phillip," he answered.

"Well, Prince Phillip, meet Princess Aurora," Flittle said.

Maleficent didn't have to be in the room to know that as Flittle stepped aside, Phillip would see Aurora and his eyes would widen as recognized her from the forest.

Sure enough, his next words were "I know this girl."

Not satisfied only to listen in on the events unfolding, Maleficent stepped out of the shadows. The two guards had only a moment to recognize the horns before Maleficent lifted her staff and quickly knocked them out. Turning, she gestured to Diaval to follow her.

Silently, they slipped through the open door. A huge bed dominated the center of the room, heavy curtains draped on either side of the massive headboard. Intricate carvings were etched into the four wooden posts that held up the bed. And flowing down from the top, covering the now sleeping form of Aurora, was a thin white translucent fabric that made Maleficent think of a spider's web. Seemingly weak, but actually strong enough to keep things trapped inside.

Glancing around the rest of the room, Maleficent felt a wave of sadness flood over her. This was clearly the room that had once been intended as Aurora's nursery. A small crib, the same translucent fabric covering it, was pushed against one of the three giant windows that lined the far wall. But while the large bed was clean, the crib was covered in a thick layer of dust, as were the toys and rocking horse pushed into the far corner.

This is my doing, Maleficent thought, gazing around the sad room. This was where Aurora would have spent hours playing, reading with her mother, pouring tea with her imaginary friends. *But I took that from her. I even took her chance of happiness in the Moors away from her. And now she lies here, lifeless. And I have no one to blame but myself.*

Shaking her head, Maleficent moved a bit closer, careful not to make any noise that would alert the pixies or Phillip. There was still a small chance, a very small chance, that all was not lost. But it depended on something intangible.

"Why is she sleeping?" Phillip asked, unaware of Maleficent's arrival.

"She's trapped in an enchantment," Knotgrass answered.

Maleficent rolled her eyes. The three pixies were hopeless. Phillip knew nothing of magic. Telling him it was an enchantment could frighten him away.

Luckily, it didn't seem to faze Phillip. He took a step closer to Aurora. "She's the most beautiful girl I've ever seen," he said.

The three pixies exchanged excited glances. "Do you want to kiss her?" Thistlewit asked.

Phillip nodded. "Very much."

"Go on, then," Knotgrass said, gesturing toward the bed.

"I wouldn't feel right about it," Phillip said, hesitating. "I barely know her. We only met once."

In the shadows, Maleficent's heart began to pound. He *had* to kiss her. He *had* to! The faeries couldn't let him walk out the door just because he was being a gentleman. This could be their last chance. This could be true love! Feeling Diaval's gaze on her, she turned and shot him a look. She knew what he was thinking. He was thinking *I told you so. True Love's Kiss can exist.* But she didn't even care. Hope was flowing through her, pushing aside the old, hard skepticism that had filled her for years.

Luckily, the pixies had no intention of letting Phillip walk out of the room just yet.

Flittle pushed the prince closer. "Haven't you ever heard of love at first sight?"

"Kiss her!" Knotgrass urged.

Slowly, Phillip leaned down and gently moved aside the light fabric. Maleficent's breath caught in her throat as she waited for him to close his eyes, pucker his lips . . .

Then he leaned back up. "An enchantment, you say?"

Maleficent nearly cried out in frustration. At the same time, the pixies shouted, "Kiss her!" and, together, pushed him back down.

For a moment, Phillip struggled, and Maleficent felt panic rise in her throat. But then he stopped fighting and, once more, leaned down.

And then, ever so slowly, he gently kissed her.

It was the perfect kiss. Soft, sweet, full of unspoken promises. It was the kiss girls dreamed of as they lay in bed at night. It was the kiss poems were written about. It was the kiss of fairy tales and romance. Maleficent couldn't have imagined such a perfect kiss sixteen years earlier when she cursed an innocent babe.

But it didn't matter how perfect the kiss was or how much love Phillip felt.

Aurora didn't wake up.

CHAPTER TWENTY-THREE

"Is something supposed to happen now?" Phillip stood up straight and looked at the pixies expectantly.

Maleficent's heart sank. Hope fled and all the bitterness and despair that she had pushed aside in that moment as Phillip's and Aurora's lips met came flooding back. She should have known. True love didn't exist. Aurora would never wake up. Maleficent would never be able to explain herself. They would never be able to walk through the Moors together, never watch a sunset or play with the snow faeries in their meadow. Aurora would sleep on . . . forever. Maleficent suddenly realized that her parents ultimately had been right—there really were good humans out there, ones who appreciated and loved nature as much as the faeries did. She realized that peace was possible between the races, that humans didn't need to be dealt with violently. But she'd come to this realization far too late.

Near the bed, the three pixies threw up their hands in frustration. They were upset as well, but for more selfish reasons. If King Stefan found out they had failed to wake up his daughter, there was no telling what he would do to them.

"I was certain he was the one," Flittle said to the others as she pushed Phillip out the door.

Following him, Knotgrass nodded. "We have to keep looking. Scrape the bottom of the barrel. He doesn't have to be a prince. He doesn't even have to be handsome."

"Or even that clean," Thistlewit added as they moved into the hallway and shut the door behind them.

Stepping out of her hiding spot in the shadows of the bedroom, Maleficent made her way to the bed. Sinking at Aurora's side, she looked at the beautiful princess. Even asleep, she looked kind and good, and Maleficent was racked anew with guilt for the punishment she had foolishly inflicted on the innocent girl. Who would have thought, all those long years before, that things would turn out that way? That the curse would be as great a punishment for Maleficent as it was for Aurora.

Letting out a deep, sad sigh, she reached out and gently brushed a strand of Aurora's hair from her face. Diaval stood at her side, his silent presence a small comfort to Maleficent. She took a deep breath and spoke softly, her voice cracking with emotion. "I will not ask you for forgiveness. What I have done is unforgivable. I was so lost in hatred and revenge. I never dreamed that I could love you so much. You stole what was left of my heart. And now I've lost you forever." She paused, wiping a tear. "But I swear, no harm will come to you as long as I live . . . and not a day shall pass that I won't miss your smile. . . ."

Maleficent's voice trailed off. There was nothing left she could say or do. This was the only good-bye she would ever get. And she wanted to make it count. Leaning over, she placed one hand over Aurora's and gently kissed the girl on the forehead.

A surge of magic filled the room.

And then Aurora's eyes fluttered open.

Maleficent let out a gasp as the princess's calm blue eyes met her unsure green ones. She was so happy that the girl was awake, but scared that Aurora was still angry.

"Hello, Godmother," Aurora said, beaming up at Maleficent, her smile bringing new light to the room.

Maleficent's throat constricted as her body was racked with emotion. Aurora was awake. And she didn't hate her.

But how could it be? Why had her kiss worked and not Phillip's? And then Maleficent smiled as realization swept over her like a wave. She had been so focused on the love that had broken her heart that she had never stopped to think there was an even deeper, truer love: that of a mother and daughter. That was what Aurora had become to her—a daughter. She loved her unconditionally, without question. She would love her on the bad days and on the great days. When Aurora was near and when she was far. She would love her for the woman she would become and the girl she was now.

That, Maleficent realized as she looked at Aurora's huge smile, was the truest of loves.

Bursting with happiness, Maleficent smiled back. "Hello, beastie."

Maleficent didn't waste any time filling Aurora in on what had happened since she had pricked her finger. The girl listened closely as Maleficent told her about the pixies' mission to find a prince to wake her and how they had failed. She even told her about the valiant effort Phillip had made. While she had wanted to skip it, a knowing look from Diaval changed her mind. It was only fair, after all the lies that had been told, to speak the truth. Aurora was going to face a tough decision in the days to come—whether to stay with her father or be with Maleficent—and she deserved all the information before she made up her mind.

When Maleficent was finished, Aurora didn't say anything. She simply nodded and slowly sat up. Then, with Maleficent's help, she shakily got to her feet. Now that she was awake, she wanted to speak to her father.

Making their way out of the room, they found the hall deserted. The two guards were gone and the lights along the wall had been blown out. With a growing sense of dread, Maleficent and Diaval, now a raven, led Aurora down one hall after another. They descended a long, winding staircase and moved past the iron thorns and brambles that had burned Maleficent earlier. Aurora's eyes grew wide as she took in the sharp objects she hadn't noticed before, clearly placed there by her father. While Aurora didn't say it, Maleficent knew the girl was scared. And with good reason. This did not look like the castle of fairy tales and happy endings. It was a dark and evil place, vibrating with hate.

Finally, they reached the balcony that looked down over the Great Hall. The huge room was dark save for a single pool of light that illuminated the center. Cautiously, they moved down the stairs and closer to the light.

Maleficent kept her gaze straight ahead, focused on the two large thrones just visible in the shadows. They were the same thrones where Stefan and his queen had sat while their infant daughter was showered with gifts at her christening. The same thrones that had borne witness to Maleficent's curse and the terrible aftermath. Now they once more sat there, silent witnesses. But to what? Maleficent wondered. What did they know that she did not?

As Maleficent turned to make sure Aurora was okay, her eyes grew wide. The girl was gone. But where? She had been there just a moment before. Turning, Maleficent frantically scanned the empty room. "Aurora?" she called out. From the darkness, she heard the muffled sound of someone trying to speak. "Aurora!" Maleficent cried out, racing toward the sound.

Finding herself in the middle of the circle of light, Maleficent paused, uncertain. Something didn't feel right. With a growing sense of dread, she looked up. And then she gulped. Hanging there, right above her head, was a giant iron net.

Before she could move, the net fell toward her. Dropping her staff, Maleficent raised her hands above her head to try to block it. But it was no use. The moment the iron touched her exposed flesh, she felt a searing pain and heard the sizzle as her skin burned. Unable to handle the intense pain, Maleficent fell to her knees, the net covering her the way her wings used to. But while her wings had brought her comfort then, the net now just brought her misery.

Her breath coming in gasps, Maleficent was barely aware of the footsteps of a dozen men as Stefan's soldiers surrounded her. They prodded the net with long spears, causing the iron to move against Maleficent and find new pieces of skin to burn. She clenched her jaw, convinced it couldn't get any worse. And then, through the fog of pain, she heard Aurora cry out.

"Don't kill her!" the princess shouted.

Raising her head slightly, Maleficent saw that Stefan had arrived and was now holding Aurora out in front of him. It had been a long time since Maleficent had seen Stefan, and she was shocked by how drastically he had deteriorated. His sunken cheeks were red, and his shoulders stooped. The thick hair he had always worn long was thinning and gray. And the eyes that stared down at Maleficent were bloodshot and empty.

An evil smile slowly spread across Stefan's face as his fingers dug into the soft flesh of Aurora's arm. Maleficent cringed. Stefan had completely lost it. He had been intent on destroying Maleficent for so long that he didn't even realize he was hurting his own daughter. In fact, he seemed annoyed by her, and when she pleaded once more for him to stop hurting Maleficent, Stefan pushed her backward. The force of the shove threw Aurora to the ground. From where she lay, she looked up in horror, shocked by her father's violence.

Desperate to save Aurora from any more pain or disappointment, Maleficent tried to move under the net. But it was no use. The iron was doing its job, and with every passing moment she grew weaker. If only there was something else she could do. Some other way out of this horrific situation . . .

And then she heard Diaval's familiar caw.

Despite the pain that continued to wash over her in waves, Maleficent smiled. Yes, she thought, that would work. That would work quite nicely. Softly, she began to mutter.

There was a swoosh of magic and the curtains on the windows blew as wind filled the Great Hall. And then, as Stefan and his soldiers watched, Diaval began to transform. His wings grew longer, the black feathers replaced by dark scales, until they spanned nearly the entire length of the hall. His beak became a large snout with a mouth full of sharp teeth, and his neck extended so that the top of his head nearly grazed the ceiling. And his two feet turned into long, powerful, scale-covered legs. On the end of each foot, giant razor-sharp claws dug into the stone floor. Rearing back his head, Diaval let out a loud roar. Before the terrified soldiers stood something they had never seen before, something that even this magical land had thought to be a myth. Diaval had become a dragon.

Maleficent raised her head and watched as a stunned Stefan took a step back. If the pain hadn't been so over-whelming, she would have smiled to see him struck down with fear. Then she turned her head slightly and saw that Aurora had climbed to her feet and was running away. As she watched, the girl disappeared up the long staircase that led to the tower. And then Maleficent did allow herself a smile. Because no matter what happened next, no matter what pain Stefan inflicted on Maleficent, or Diaval inflicted on Stefan, Aurora wouldn't be there to witness it. She would be saved from that horror. And after everything the girl had gone through, one less horror was a priceless gift.

CHAPTER TWENTY-FOUR

As Aurora made her escape, Diaval continued to wreak havoc on the Great Hall. With a swish of his tail, he knocked down a line of soldiers. He let out a roar, raining fire down on another group. As he raised his head, the two large horns that dominated his forehead smashed into one of the large chandeliers, shattering it into a thousand pieces. The broken crystal fell on the soldiers still on their feet, causing them to scream in pain.

Under the net, Maleficent stayed curled in a helpless ball, weakening every moment she spent surrounded by the iron. Her staff was too far away to reach, and without it, she felt even more powerless. After a while, she could only lie there and listen as Diaval roared. She could only lie there and do nothing as soldiers stumbled past her, trying to escape the fire-breathing dragon. She could only lie there and think, *This is all my fault.*

The minutes seemed to stretch on for hours, and Maleficent began to think she might never escape her iron prison. Then, through the haze of pain that continued to rack her body, Maleficent heard the sound of approaching footsteps. Unlike the hurried, frightened ones of the soldiers, these footsteps were determined, confident. She looked up, already knowing who she would see.

Stefan was approaching, his eyes glued on Maleficent, trapped under the net. They bore into her, all traces of the feelings he had once had for her gone. For the first time, Maleficent truly saw him for the despicable man he had become. True, she knew he had changed physically— the boyish build and unlined face replaced by girth and wrinkles. And she knew he had grown colder. That was evidenced by his murdering King Henry and cutting off her wings, to name a few offenses. But before, those things had made her hate him even more. Now she felt almost sorry for him.

There was nothing left of the boy she had fallen in love with in the Moors. No hint of the playfulness that Stefan had easily displayed as they chatted beside the bogs or walked through the forest. This man before her was hard, cold, and dead inside. The years of building iron walls around his castle had had an adverse effect—they had caused him to build an iron wall around his heart. Staring into his eyes, Maleficent felt sad. Sad and frightened. For there was no telling what he would do now. Desperately, she reached for her staff again. But it was still just out of her grasp.

Seeing her struggle, Stefan smiled cruelly. "I still regret not killing you that night," he said harshly.

The words cut deep and any sadness she had begun to feel for Stefan vanished in an instant. Memories of that night long before, when he had taken her heart and her wings, came flooding back. He might as well have killed her for the damage he had done. That night had set in motion a horrible chain of events. In a way, that night had made her a heartless monster just like him—until she met Aurora and things began to change. Yet she would never admit that to him. Not now. So instead, Maleficent gathered her remaining strength and said, "You were always weak."

Stefan's face turned red and his hand tightened around the hilt of his sword. Maleficent knew she had gone too far. But what did it matter now? The chances of her escaping were far from good. As if to prove her right, Stefan raised his heavy sword high above his head. Then, with a loud scream, he brought it down. . . .

Maleficent closed her eyes, waiting for the blow.

But it never came.

Instead, there was a roar followed by a loud thud. Opening her eyes, Maleficent saw Stefan lying on the floor a few feet away, and standing above her was Diaval the dragon. She smiled at him as he lowered his long neck and gently grabbed the iron net in his teeth. Then he pulled it off Maleficent, freeing her at last.

As soon as the net was gone, Maleficent grabbed her staff and scrambled to her feet. As the blood rushed back to her limbs, a wave of dizziness hit her, forcing her to steady herself on her staff for a moment. Taking a few deep breaths, she waited for her head to clear. Then she stood up straight. Adrenaline flooded through her as she took in the chaos around her. Soldiers were running in every direction, fearful of the giant creature in their midst. Diaval had broken nearly every chandelier in the Great Hall and his fiery breath had scorched the walls, turning them black. His giant claws had left deep gashes in the stone floor, while his long tail had taken out several large pillars near the hall's grand entrance. Scanning the room, she saw Stefan struggling to his feet, and without hesitation, he began to charge toward her. But he didn't make it far. Diaval stepped between them and, with another mighty roar, renewed his fight with Stefan and the soldiers.

Using the distraction, Maleficent raced toward the stairs unnoticed. She needed to find Aurora . . . immediately.

As Maleficent reached the top of the stairs, she turned back. She watched as Diaval hissed and snapped at the men, trying to keep them at bay. But more and more soldiers came. They had sharp weapons and he was not used to his dragon body. She saw panic in his eyes as he whipped his tail, knocking a few more men down. Then Diaval turned toward the far wall. Racing forward, he smashed through it, sending the iron plates on the other side to the ground. Through the gaping hole, Maleficent could make out one of the castle's many towers nearby. Its rounded sides offered no footholds, so the soldiers had no way of climbing it. But Diaval's claws could easily dig into the stone. Seeing his chance to escape, Diaval began to climb up the tower wall and disappeared from view a moment later.

Maleficent turned and frantically looked around. Where could Aurora have gone? There was a long hall to her right and another to her left. But straight ahead, slightly swaying, was a huge door. That had to be it. Racing through, Maleficent found herself in front of another set of stairs. They circled up, up, and up, leading high into the tower that at that very moment Diaval was scaling.

Quickly, Maleficent began to climb the stairs, her heart pounding with the fear of what she might find. Aurora didn't know the castle. She didn't know the soldiers or the cruelty angry men were capable of expressing. She had lived her entire life protected from such things. And now she had been thrown right into the middle, witness to some of the worst acts of human nature. Maleficent ached at the thought of Aurora frightened and alone, wandering the castle halls. Her footsteps quickened, and finally, she reached the room at the top of the tower. It was empty. On the far side of the room, a door led out to a long bridge that connected the tower with the one next to it. And standing there, in the middle of the bridge, was Aurora. Sighing with relief, Maleficent ran out.

But her relief was short-lived.

From behind her, she heard a whish, and then she felt a familiar pain rack her body. Looking over her shoulder, she saw Stefan. He had a long iron whip in his hand and a crazed look in his eyes. He took a step forward, lashing the whip over and over in front of him. Raising her staff, Maleficent stood her ground. She was not going to let him defeat her, not now. Not when Aurora was so close. Narrowing her eyes in determination, Maleficent took a step forward, swinging her staff.

The sound of iron against wood rang out on the bridge as Stefan lashed his whip repeatedly. And over and over again, Maleficent deflected the blows with her staff. They moved forward and backward, their motions a terrifying mockery of a romantic waltz. The fight took them from the bridge onto another, neither of them backing down, both of them determined to win. Maleficent forgot that Aurora was nearby. Forgot that she had come to save her. All she could think about was defeating Stefan once and for all. Making him pay for the pain he had caused her and his daughter. Her mind went blank with rage and she slammed her staff into Stefan.

They were so engrossed in their fight that neither noticed the ground beneath their feet was shaking.

Nor did they notice that Diaval was still clinging to the tower, scrambling toward the roof and sending debris and iron plummeting to the ground far below. And they definitely didn't notice that standing on a smaller bridge right underneath them was Aurora. The princess stood helplessly as broken pieces of the tower slammed into her bridge, causing it to shake violently.

And then Aurora's bridge collapsed.

Maleficent heard an ear-piercing scream, and her rage vanished, instantly replaced by fear. Turning, she saw Aurora falling. The girl's arms flailed as she tried to slow her fall. But it was useless. The ground was quickly approaching. Maleficent frantically looked around for some way to help her beloved Aurora. But there was nothing she could do. Her magic wasn't powerful enough and she didn't have the wings to fly. And then she noticed Diaval and felt a surge of hope. The girl meant as much to him as she did to Maleficent. He was not going to let her die. As Diaval perched on the roof of the tower, his eyes were glued to Aurora. He judged the distance and then, with a mighty flap of his huge wings, launched himself from the roof and swooped down after Aurora.

Maleficent's heart stopped as she watched Diaval's huge black body speed down after Aurora's small pale one. He stretched his neck, going faster and faster. Then he reached out his claws and closed them around Aurora, swooping safely back up right before they both hit the ground.

Air flooded into Maleficent's lungs and her heart began to beat once more as she watched the two land safely nearby. That had been too close for comfort. If Diaval had been just one second slower . . .

Whish!

Maleficent let out a cry as Stefan's iron-chain whip wrapped around her arm. Unprepared for the pain, Maleficent lost her grip on her staff. She watched helplessly as it fell over the edge of the bridge.

Seeing that she no longer had a way to defend herself, Stefan let out an evil laugh. He began to lash her. Raising her hands in front of her face, Maleficent tried to duck out of the way. But the whip kept coming. Taking a few steps back, she let out a gasp as her foot found air instead of ground. Looking over her shoulder, she saw that she was backed up against the edge of the bridge. There was nowhere left to go.

As she turned back, her eyes met Stefan's. *So this is how it will end,* Maleficent thought sadly, looking at the king's evil grin. All the years of hate and battles. The walls that had been built, of iron and thorn. They had all been for naught. They had not been the things to destroy either Maleficent or Stefan. In the end, it would be a fall. A fall into nothing. Letting out a sigh, Maleficent waited for the inevitable. She watched as Stefan's smile grew broader and broader as he waited for the inevitable, as well.

And then his smile vanished.

Behind her, Maleficent heard a whoosh, and then she felt something she hadn't felt in many, many years. It was a feeling of comfort, of wholeness. It was a feeling almost as strong as the love she felt for Aurora. A smile began to spread across her face as she slowly turned around.

There, hovering in the air, were her wings.

They were as strong and beautiful as they had been on the day Stefan took them from her, and Maleficent let out a soft cry. How could this be? she wondered. Had they been there, in the castle, all along? And if they had been, how had they been released? Looking down, she saw Aurora and suddenly knew just how they had come back to her. Somehow, Aurora had found the missing piece of her. With a huge smile, Maleficent turned back to her wings and opened her arms.

There was an earth-shattering crack and Maleficent disappeared in a magical explosion of light. When the light faded, Maleficent and her wings were one once more. With a mighty flap, she lifted herself high in the air and hovered, glorying in the moment. She had never believed this day would come. Yet it had. And now she was close to having everything she needed and wanted in the world.

While she wanted to fly high into the air and forget the problems below while she dipped and soared on the wind, once again free to go wherever she pleased, there was one last thing to take care of.

Swooping down, she slammed Stefan with one of her powerful wings. The king was thrown back, stumbling as he tried to keep his footing. Flying forward, Maleficent held him up against the tower wall. She leaned forward, her face mere inches from Stefan's.

"You won't kill me," Stefan said, trying to sound brave but failing. "I'm her father."

For a moment, Maleficent didn't say anything. She just stared at Stefan, struggling with herself. She had never wanted to hurt someone as much as she wanted to hurt Stefan. He deserved it. That she was sure of. Yet before he had betrayed her, Maleficent had never believed in revenge. She had never wanted to hurt anyone or anything. Stefan had changed all that the day he broke her heart. But if she killed him now, wouldn't that be letting him get the best of her? Wouldn't that, in a way, be letting him win? Aurora could forgive her for a lot, but would she be able to forgive her for killing her father?

With a sigh, Maleficent released Stefan, landing and taking a step back. She waited, wondering if this act of kindness would restore anything of the man she once cared for. But instead, he said, "I want you to know that I never loved you."

Maleficent let out a bitter laugh. "Oh, Stefan," she replied. "You never were a good liar."

There was nothing left to be said or done. Maleficent turned and began to walk away. But hearing the sound of running footsteps, she whipped around just in time to see Stefan racing toward her, an iron knife gripped in his hand. A moment later, he slammed into her, and together, they fell off the bridge.

The moonlight silhouetted their bodies as Maleficent and Stefan plummeted toward the ground. Maleficent's wings were cupped around them, almost like an opaque hammock, preventing those below from witnessing their fight. The king struggled against the wings as he tried to stab Maleficent. In turn, she ducked and wove to elude the weapon, causing their fall to take on an erratic pattern. But while she managed to avoid the knife, she wouldn't be able to avoid the ground, which was rapidly approaching.

As Stefan raised the knife once more, Maleficent flipped over. The sudden movement caused the king to lose his grip, and before she could grab him, Stefan fell out of her arms.

A moment later, his body hit the ground and lay there, lifeless.

Opening her wings, Maleficent slowed her fall and rose into the air. Then, seeing Stefan on the ground, she swept low and landed next to him. Bowing her head, she closed her eyes, a myriad of emotions coursing through her.

The person lying on the ground next to her was the first person to have loved her. The first person she had loved. And for that, she felt grateful. For without any understanding of love, she could never have opened her heart to Aurora. But this person was also the first to have betrayed her and the reason she had closed her heart for so long. He had been her blessing and her curse. And now he was no more. She felt a deep sadness. But after a moment, she realized it was sadness not for her, but for Aurora. For the girl would never have the chance to know her father.

As Maleficent raised her head, her eyes met Aurora's. The girl stood a bit away, her face pale. But meeting Maleficent's gaze, she nodded. And in that nod, Maleficent knew that Aurora would be fine. She would forgive Maleficent for her part in this, and she would live a happy life, surrounded by beauty, nature, and loved ones. And Maleficent would be there to guide her and protect her . . . always. She had found her family once more. And it was in a kindred spirit. A human girl.

Epilogue

THE MOORS WERE ABUZZ WITH EXCITEMENT. THE WALLERBOGS BURBLED AND GURGLED MORE MUD. THE DEW FAERIES FLEW FROM LEAF TO LEAF, LEAVING SPARKLING WATER SHINING LIKE DIAMONDS IN THEIR WAKE. IN THE STREAMS, THE WATER FAERIES PREENED MORE THAN USUAL. The rest of the Fair Folk headed straight for the Faerie Mound. Today was the big day, and they did not want to miss anything.

Maleficent stood in front of the throne on the Mound, smiling at the familiar faces around her. Diaval stood at her side. Nearby, Sweetpea winked at her, and Robin positively beamed. Maleficent felt so grateful they were all there. Her family.

A rustle in the brush alerted them that their guest of honor had arrived. Maleficent turned her head to see Aurora striding toward the Mound, a halo of sunlit hair glowing around her face. The flowers bloomed excitedly as Aurora passed them, and the hovering sparrows chirped happily. She stopped in front of Maleficent, grinning at her faerie godmother. Maleficent's eyes welled with proud tears.

"Oh, there she is! Hurry up! They're waiting!" Knotgrass's shrill voice came from the other side of the Mound. The crowd turned to see Knotgrass and Flittle zigzagging toward them with a gleaming crown in tow.

"Wait for me!" Thistlewit called, trailing behind them.

As soon as the three pixies reached Maleficent and Aurora, they paused midair, gasping dramatically to catch their breath. Maleficent restrained herself from rolling her eyes. Finally, Knotgrass spoke.

"We present this crown to our little Aurora, for whom we have sacrificed the best years of our—" She coughed, stopping her speech as soon as she saw the glare Maleficent was giving her.

Maleficent knew it was time to take matters in her own hands. *Never send a pixie to do a faerie godmother's job*, she thought, taking the crown from Knotgrass. Then, ever so gently, she placed it upon Aurora's head.

"You have your queen," Maleficent announced to the crowd. A joyous cheer erupted. Maleficent watched Aurora smile warmly, a smile that only grew as she saw Phillip approach the throne. Maleficent watched as Aurora greeted the border guards, shaking their wooden hands, officially forming a new allegiance. It was all Maleficent's parents had wanted—peace and harmony. The scene overwhelmed Maleficent.

Aurora would make a great and noble queen. One to unite the lands and bring the humans and Fair Folk together.

But, as many thought whenever they saw the graceful figure soaring through the air, it took a great hero and a terrible villain to make it all come about. And her name was Maleficent.

SEP 1 6

Tualatin Public Library
18878 SW Martinazzi Avenue
Tualatin, OR 97062-7092
Member of Washington County Cooperative Library Services

WITHDRAWN

CLIMATE
On the Move in a Warming World
MIGRANTS

REBECCA E. HIRSCH

TWENTY-FIRST CENTURY BOOKS / MINNEAPOLIS

This book is dedicated to all the people who are
losing their homes because of climate change
—R.E.H.

Text copyright © 2017 by Lerner Publishing Group, Inc.

All rights reserved. International copyright secured. No part of this book may be reproduced, stored in
a retrieval system, or transmitted in any form or by any means—electronic, mechanical, photocopying,
recording, or otherwise—without the prior written permission of Lerner Publishing Group, Inc., except for
the inclusion of brief quotations in an acknowledged review.

Twenty-First Century Books
A division of Lerner Publishing Group, Inc.
241 First Avenue North
Minneapolis, MN 55401 USA

For reading levels and more information, look up this title at www.lernerbooks.com.

Main body text set in ITC Officina Serif Std Book 11/15.
Typeface provided by Adobe Systems.

Library of Congress Cataloging-in-Publication Data

Names: Hirsch, Rebecca E., author.
Title: Climate migrants : on the move in a warming world / by Rebecca E. Hirsch.
Description: Minneapolis : Twenty-First Century Books, [2016] | Audience: Ages 11–19. | Audience: Grades 9
    to 12. | Includes bibliographical references and index.
Identifiers: LCCN 2015035715| ISBN 9781467793414 (lb : alk. paper) | ISBN 9781512411454 (eb pdf : alk.
    paper)
Subjects: LCSH: Human beings—Migrations—Juvenile literature. | Emigration and immigration—Juvenile
    literature. | Climatic changes—Juvenile literature. | Global warming—Juvenile literature. | Social
    ecology—Juvenile literature.
Classification: LCC GN370 .H57 2016 | DDC 304.8—dc23

LC record available at http://lccn.loc.gov/2015035715

Manufactured in the United States of America
1-38380-20288-3/22/2016